"Just to be safe, maybe you shouldn't be alone," Danny said.

Carrie glanced at him. "Oh, I don't think Ted would hurt me."

"You said yourself he was furious. And he blamed you for putting him on the spot."

She huffed out a breath. "You have a point, but don't worry. Like I said before, it's rare that I'm ever alone. So I guess I'm safe."

"You're alone with me now."

Silence. She turned to look at him. "I am, aren't I?" Her lips curved into a slow smile. "But you don't scare me, Danny."

"That's good." He settled back into his seat. He'd never tell her, but when he was being honest, she scared him, just a little. She unsettled him and made him think about her in a way he had never thought about another woman. As if the thought of her being hurt by anyone caused a physical pain.

Danny wasn't that kind of man, but it seemed with Carrie, he was...

CLOSE CALL IN COLORADO

CINDI MYERS

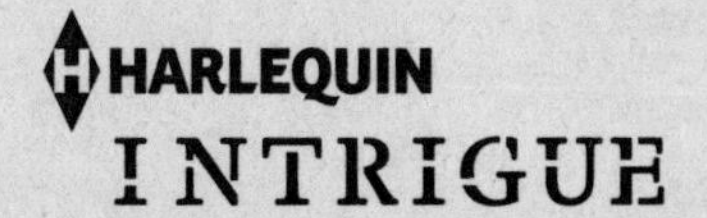

Recycling programs for this product may not exist in your area.

ISBN-13: 978-1-335-58242-3

Close Call in Colorado

For questions and comments about the quality of this book, please contact us at CustomerService@Harlequin.com.

Harlequin Enterprises ULC
22 Adelaide St. West, 41st Floor
Toronto, Ontario M5H 4E3, Canada
www.Harlequin.com

Printed in U.S.A.

Cindi Myers is the author of more than fifty novels. When she's not plotting new romance story lines, she enjoys skiing, gardening, cooking, crafting and daydreaming. A lover of small-town life, she lives with her husband and two spoiled dogs in the Colorado mountains.

Books by Cindi Myers

Harlequin Intrigue

Eagle Mountain Search and Rescue

Eagle Mountain Cliffhanger
Canyon Kidnapping
Mountain Terror
Close Call in Colorado

Eagle Mountain: Search for Suspects

Disappearance at Dakota Ridge
Conspiracy in the Rockies
Missing at Full Moon Mine
Grizzly Creek Standoff

The Ranger Brigade: Rocky Mountain Manhunt

Investigation in Black Canyon
Mountain of Evidence
Mountain Investigation
Presumed Deadly

Eagle Mountain Murder Mystery: Winter Storm Wedding

Ice Cold Killer
Snowbound Suspicion
Cold Conspiracy
Snowblind Justice

Visit the Author Profile page at Harlequin.com.

CAST OF CHARACTERS

Carrie Andrews—A successful architect and single mother of two children, Carrie must step into the role of SAR captain when someone threatens everyone in the organization and the culprit may be one of the other volunteers.

Danny Irwin—A longtime SAR volunteer and RN, Danny has a reputation as an easygoing ladies' man who is only out for a good time. But when an unknown assailant threatens SAR—and Carrie—he reveals another side of his personality.

Ted Carruthers—One of the founding members of the organization, Ted is dedicated, but lately he's been having trouble keeping up with the demands of the work. He doesn't take kindly to the prospect of being sidelined.

Austen Morrissey—The rookie volunteer was once saved by SAR and has joined the organization to pay back that debt.

Tony Meisner—The SAR captain's near-fatal accident during a training exercise is the first of several incidents designed to destroy the organization.

Chapter One

On the list of activities Carrie Andrews would like to be doing on a frigid March Saturday, rappelling into an icy canyon didn't even make the top twenty. Yet here she was, standing on the edge of the canyon wall, in helmet, climbing harness and crampons, awaiting her turn to complete the descent as part of a required training exercise with Eagle Mountain Search and Rescue.

"I'll send you down as soon as Tony and Danny are safely at the bottom." Training officer Sheri Stevens came to stand beside Carrie. A tall blonde who regularly competed in—and won—ice climbing competitions, Sheri thrived on this kind of thing. Like several others on the search and rescue team, she made dangerous exercises like this one look easy.

Carrie clapped her gloved hands together, trying to force more warmth into her fingers. "I don't know why I always get so nervous about these climbs," she said. "I've done them dozens of times."

"Just remember your training and take your time," Sheri said. "Safety is way more important than speed, even in real-life situations where an injured person is awaiting rescue down there. You can't help someone if you don't get to them safely."

Carrie nodded. "I know." But after five years with the team, she also had a mental catalogue full of terrible climbing accidents they had responded to—a graphically illustrated memory bank of everything that could go wrong.

She forced her attention back to the two men currently rappelling into the canyon. SAR captain Tony Meisner descended swiftly, comfortable enough to use both hands to navigate around icy outcroppings, relying on his harness and the Prusik loop that provided a backup to the belay loop to keep him safe, whereas Carrie was never able to let go of her death grip on the rope as she descended.

Positioned several yards over from Tony, Danny Irwin was a more tentative climber. Like Carrie, he had trained extensively and could be counted on in an emergency to do everything required, but he wasn't one to climb for enjoyment. Fun and easygoing on the ground, he was all business when it came to anything dangerous. A nurse in his day job, he had a reputation as a bit of a player, having dated every single woman on the team except Carrie, who had turned down his overtures when she first joined SAR five years previously. He hadn't pressed the issue, and they worked well together on the team, but they weren't close.

"Tony is really booking it today," Sheri said. She moved over to get a better look. "He's almost to that last tricky part where the canyon wall juts out."

"Why did he choose that route?" Carrie shifted closer to Sheri. "Why not move over where he doesn't have to negotiate around that spot?"

"He said he wanted a challenge." Sheri shrugged. "You know Tony. He does things his own way."

"I guess it's good practice for difficult situations we might get into," Carrie said. "But still, I—"

A shout went up from within the canyon. Carrie stared in horror as Tony's rope hurtled into the chasm below. "What's going on?" Sheri rushed to the edge of the canyon and dropped to her knees to look down.

"What is it?" Carrie asked, and hurried to Sheri's side.

"Tony's fallen." Rookie Austen Morrissey joined them, his face ashen. The thirty-something had signed up with the team several months before, after relocating to Eagle Mountain. His expression reflected all the horror Carrie felt. "Everything looked fine and then…the rope just came loose."

SHOUTING DISTRACTED DANNY from focusing on the descent. He steadied himself and turned his head to look across and down at Tony, who had been climbing ten yards away, skimming down the icy rock with his usual flair. Except Tony wasn't there. The ropes he had been using in his descent were no longer there, and Danny's heart rose into his throat. "Tony!" he shouted. "Tony!"

"What happened?" Sheri called down, using a battery-operated hailer. "Where is Tony?"

"I don't know!" Danny looked up his own ropes,

momentarily frozen. He had made similar climbs dozens of times in training and in real-life rescues, but he was never entirely comfortable. As a registered nurse, his chief role in search and rescue was to deliver medical aid, but he strove to be as physically competent as he could be, too. He never wanted to be the weak link in any rescue operation. But he didn't have the natural talent people like Tony and Sheri seemed to have.

"Get down there and see if you can find him!" Sheri shouted.

The order got him moving. Danny focused on completing the descent as quickly as possible, his mind running through all the possibilities. The last time he had checked, Tony had been about fifteen feet deeper into the canyon than Danny was. Which meant he had fallen—what—twenty yards? Thirty? Had he had his crampons set in the ice at the time he fell? He forced himself to look over, half-expecting to see his friend hanging head down, leg bones snapped by the force of the fall. But he saw nothing except empty ice-and-snow-covered rock.

He tried to tell himself that was a good sign, but he only felt sick inside. There was a lot of rock and ice between the place where he had last seen Tony and the bottom of the canyon—lots of tree branches and rock outcroppings he could bash against or be snagged by. He divided his attention between his own descent and checking to his right for signs of Tony, but he saw nothing.

Nothing, that is, until he was almost to the canyon

floor. Then he looked down and saw what at first appeared to be a pile of discarded clothing on the edge of a trickle of icy water from Grizzly Creek where it flowed through the canyon. He made himself move faster, though still methodically, until his crampon-shod boots crunched onto the canyon floor. He fumbled releasing himself from the ropes, then hurried toward his friend, shedding his pack as he went.

He dropped to his knees beside Tony, who lay with his legs bent under him, face bone white beneath his beard. The ropes he'd been using to descend—red-and-yellow climbing ropes—were still fastened to his harness and lay in a tangle over and around him. "Tony, it's Danny. Can you hear me?" He unpacked medical gear as he spoke, even as the radio mounted on his shoulder squawked.

"What's going on down there?" Sheri demanded. As training officer, she was leading today's exercise.

"I've found Tony," Danny said. "He's alive. Hurt, but alive. Get a team with a litter started down right away and call for a helicopter." The canyon was too narrow to get a chopper down into. They'd have to bring Tony up in a litter, the very exercise they had been training for this morning.

He touched Tony's cheek. "Tony. It's Danny. Open your eyes for me."

Tony groaned, but opened his eyes. His pupils looked normal. His climbing helmet appeared undamaged, so maybe he hadn't hit his head on the way down. "What happened?" Danny asked. He found the pulse at Tony's wrist and started counting, eyes on his watch. The pulse was irregular but strong.

"Rope…came loose." Tony forced out the words, then groaned again as Danny began to gently examine his legs.

Danny stared. Was Tony disoriented by the fall? Basic climbing procedure was to tie a firm stopper knot at the ends of the ropes to keep them from slipping out of the anchor chain. He had heard of people forgetting this step, but Tony was always so careful. He had been a member of search and rescue for almost two decades, and had trained many other people on safe climbing techniques.

Had the rope broken? Ropes were meticulously checked before and after each use and retired after a specific number of hours, whether they appeared to be worn or not. And yet either the ropes themselves or the gear they were attached to had failed to do their job. He shook his head and focused on assessing his friend, treating him as he would any other accident victim, which meant ignoring his groans of pain as he sorted out Tony's various injuries.

By the time Hannah, Carrie, Eldon and Austen joined him in the canyon, Danny had started IV fluids and administered morphine. Hannah, a paramedic, and Carrie, second-in-command of the team, joined him, while Eldon and Austen began setting up a long line to transport the litter to the rim of the canyon.

"How's he doing?" Carrie asked. She rested a hand on Tony's shoulder.

"We won't know everything without X-rays, but

he's got fractures in both lower legs and probably one ankle. Probable rib fractures, and he may have a broken pelvis." Danny forced himself to deliver the news in a flat tone, without emotion. It was a terrible laundry list of damage and didn't begin to cover possible internal injuries.

"Let's get him immobilized and warmed against shock," Hannah said, already unpacking a thermos of hot water and several blankets.

"We need to get him untangled from these ropes," Danny said. "Give me a hand here, Eldon."

The two worked to carefully unwind the nest of ropes from around and beneath their friend. Danny worked his way to the end of the ropes, then froze, his brain not quite registering what his eyes were seeing.

"What are you staring at?" Carrie asked. She moved around to crouch next to Danny.

"Tony said the rope came loose," Danny said. "I didn't believe him. That just doesn't happen. But look." He held up the frayed and torn ends of the two ropes.

"We'll take a closer look at this later," Carrie said. "And we'll check all of them. Maybe there's some kind of defect we haven't noticed before."

Danny nodded. He hated to think of some flaw in their equipment that had escaped notice until now, but what else could it be? "Who's up top with Sheri?" he asked as he and Hannah prepared to ease Tony onto a backboard.

"Ryan and Ted are up there," Hannah said. She took out a cervical collar and began to fit it to Tony's neck. Like Sheri, Ryan was a competitive climber, though he was still recovering from injuries incurred earlier in the year. The oldest member of the force at sixty, Ted was also an experienced, capable climber, but a good person to have helping to bring the litter up to the canyon lip.

"Ted pitched a bit of a fit about staying up top," Carrie said as she positioned the backboard. "He wanted Austen to stay up there while he came down." Austen was a rookie, not as experienced with climbing. Sheri had probably wanted him to get the practice today in a real-life rescue.

"We don't need to be worrying about Ted along with Tony," Austen said. He joined them and looked down at the captain. "How's he doing?"

"He's holding on," Danny said. He didn't want to say more with Tony able to hear them. "Is the helicopter on its way?"

"Sheri was talking to the air crew when I started down," Hannah said. She was filling hot water bottles to tuck around Tony for the ride up to the top.

"What happened?" Austen asked.

"His ropes failed," Carrie said. "We don't know why yet."

"How did that happen?" Eldon leaned over Danny's shoulder to stare at Tony. "I saw him inspect all his equipment before he set up for the rappel. There was nothing wrong with the ropes then, or he wouldn't have used them."

"We'll inspect all the gear when we get back to

headquarters," Carrie said. She stood. "Are we ready to take him up?"

Hannah tugged on the straps holding Tony into the litter, and double-checked the IV line running beneath the blankets. "He's good to go."

"Let's get him on the line," Carrie said.

How many times had Danny done this, in both training exercises and real-life scenarios, fastening the litter to the line and threading the ropes through the pulleys to haul the patient up to a waiting helicopter or ambulance? Every other operation he had focused on procedure—the mechanics of making sure the trip went safely. But Tony was their captain, the leader who ran every mission. He was also a close friend. Having him seriously injured in such a freak accident rocked Danny more than he cared to admit.

He wanted to go up with Tony, but Eldon was a stronger climber, so he made the trip, leaving the rest of them to gather their gear and follow at a slower pace.

He and Carrie were the last to reach the canyon rim, arriving just as the helicopter lifted off. "They're taking him to St. Joseph's in Junction," Sheri said.

"Is here somebody we should notify?" Austen asked. "A girlfriend or his parents?"

"Tony's parents live in Florida and he doesn't have a girlfriend that I've ever heard him mention," Sheri said.

"I think we're his family," Carrie said. "I'll drive over to St. Joseph's this afternoon and see if I can get in to visit him."

"I'll go with you," Danny said.

She looked surprised. "You don't have to do that," she said.

"I want to." He clenched his hands into fists since he couldn't lash out at the anxiety that coiled in his stomach. "I was right there with him when he fell. I need to see him."

Her expression softened. "Of course." She cleared her throat. "It would be good to have some company."

He had ridden to the training exercise in the Beast, the team's aging search and rescue vehicle, but it had already pulled away without him. "You can ride with me," Carrie said as they watched the modified Jeep drive away.

He didn't especially feel like talking, but Carrie apparently needed to deal with her emotions out loud. "I still can't believe that happened," she said as she headed down the mountain road toward the town of Eagle Mountain. "Did you see him fall?"

"No." He shifted in his seat. "I don't look around all that much when I'm climbing."

"Me either," she said. "It's the part of this job I dread most."

"I don't dread it," Danny said. "It's just not the most comfortable thing." He glanced at her. She was an attractive woman, with honey-blond hair and a strong, compact frame. She was friendly, but not overly so. Self-contained, he would have said. He knew she was divorced and had a couple of little kids and worked as an architect, but she wasn't one to socialize after hours, and the one time he had asked her out she had made it clear she wasn't interested in him that way. If she was dating someone, she definitely kept that person's identity to herself.

"I don't like heights," she said. "But I make myself do it because it's part of the job."

"We've had other people join and end up quitting because something scared them," Danny said. "There's no shame in that. Not everyone is cut out for this work."

"I do it because it scares me," Carrie said. "I think it's good for me to face my fears."

Do you have a lot of fears? he wondered, but he didn't ask. Some other time he would have, but not now, with the memory of looking over and seeing empty space where Tony should have been still an icy spot in the center of his chest.

Carrie pulled her SUV into the parking area next to search and rescue headquarters and Danny followed her into the barn-like building where the others were already busy unloading gear and hanging it to dry. "Let me see Tony's ropes," he said to Carrie.

"We all want to see those ropes," Sheri said.

Carrie plopped her pack onto the table at the front of the room, and the others gathered around as she took out Tony's climbing ropes and uncoiled them.

"The ends don't look cut," Ted said. He reached out and pointed to the frayed fibers, uneven and fuzzed.

"They look more worn than anything else," Carrie said. "But the rest of the rope is in good shape."

Danny picked them up to examine the ends more closely. He ran a finger across the torn fibers, then looked along the length of the ropes. Both lines had severed near the end, just below where the stopper knot would have been. There was fuzzing in places on the rest of the rope—normal for something that was dragged across rock on a regular basis. "It looks a little discolored, on the end by where it broke," Eldon said.

"Nothing unusual about that," Sheri said. "The material fades with sun and sweat and water exposure."

"Where's the anchor chain?" Danny asked.

"I've got that." Austen stepped forward and laid the bundle of chain on the table. The stopper knot Tony had tied held firmly above the chain link, the frayed ends of the rope dangling below.

Danny brought the torn ends to his nose and sniffed. The sharp odor made his mouth pucker, as if he had tasted lemons. He turned to Eldon. "Let me see one of the other ropes," he said.

Eldon fetched a purple coil and brought it to the table. Danny laid it beside Tony's and studied the trio. The purple was a little discolored, though not as much as Tony's, but the purple rope might be newer. They were constantly replacing gear as it became too worn to be safe or reached the end of its useful life. Danny sniffed the line. It smelled of rock dust and fabric. Not lemons.

"What is it?" Carrie asked. She wasn't looking at the ropes anymore—she was studying Danny's face.

"I'm not sure." He handed her the end of one of Tony's. "What does that smell like to you?"

She brought the rope to her nose and sniffed. Her eyes widened. "It smells like acid," she said.

"What?" Sherri grabbed the line and sniffed, too. She stared at Danny. "Do you think someone poured acid on Tony's ropes?"

"I don't know." But acid would eat at the fibers and weaken them. The damage might not be noticeable until too late.

"How did acid get on the ropes?" Eldon asked. "Did he spill something on it? Some kind of cleaner or something?"

"I don't think we use anything that strong to clean," Carrie said.

"If it wasn't an accident, it was deliberate," Ted said. His face looked craggier than usual, thick gray eyebrows drawn together in a scowl.

"You mean someone did this on purpose?" Eldon asked.

"I think someone meant for Tony—or someone else—to get hurt," Ted said. "Sabotage."

Chapter Two

Sabotage. The word sent a chill through Carrie. After a long moment, she became aware of everyone looking at her. With a start she realized that, now that Tony was out of commission, it was up to her to lead the team. It wasn't a role she had ever aspired to, but it was too late to worry about that now. "Let's look at the other ropes and harnesses," she said. "See if anything else has been tampered with."

Everyone pitched in to collect the climbing gear they had used that morning and laid it out on folding tables at the front of the room. "I'm not seeing anything amiss," Sheri said.

"Nothing over here," Ted added.

"Maybe it really was an accident," Eldon said. "Something spilled on those ropes and Tony just didn't notice it."

"Maybe," Carrie said. "But Tony is usually so careful."

"We should call the hospital and see how he's doing," Sheri said.

Carrie took out her phone and found the number for St. Joseph's. The others started putting away the gear, but she knew they were listening. "I'm calling to check on a patient who was transported by helicopter this morning," Carrie explained to the woman who answered the phone. "His name is Tony Meisner and he was injured in a climbing accident in Eagle Mountain."

"Are you a family member?" the woman asked.

"No, but I—"

"I can only provide information to immediate family."

Carrie stared at the phone.

"What did they say?" Danny asked.

"She said she could only give out information to family."

"There are privacy laws," Hannah said.

"Let's go to Junction and see what we can find out in person," Danny said.

"Go," Sheri said. "We'll finish cleaning up here."

Carrie called her mom, who was looking after Carrie's two children, and let her know it would be a couple more hours before she was home, then headed for her SUV, Danny on her heels. He settled into the passenger seat, his tall frame filling the space, making her more aware of him physically. It wasn't that she didn't like Danny. He was a great guy, and a good teammate. But being near him distracted her. He was too good-looking. Too masculine for her to be entirely comfortable. Most of the time she thought of him as the playboy type, but that glimpse of raw emotion when he had talked about being with Tony when he fell had unsettled her. It made her realize there was more to Danny Irwin than flirtatious remarks and a wicked sense of humor.

"I don't think that acid spill was an accident," he said as soon as they were on the road. "Tony isn't careless like that. And whatever is on that rope, it had to be strong stuff to weaken the fibers like that."

"I wonder if we can have it tested," she said.

"Where would we do that?"

"I don't know." She ran her hands down the steering wheel. "The police?"

He made a face. "And what do we tell them? We think somebody may have sabotaged Tony's gear, but we don't know who. Or why?"

"'Who' would almost have to be someone with search and rescue," she said. The thought made her physically ill, but she couldn't think of anyone else who would have access to their gear. "But none of us would do that."

"Someone from outside could have done it," he said. "They could have come in after we left on a call."

"The building is supposed to be locked." They stored a lot of valuable equipment there, not to mention narcotics, though those were kept in a separate secured cabinet and only Danny and Hannah, as medical personnel, had the key.

"I'm not sure we're always good about locking up," Danny said. "The drugs, yeah, but you know how it is when we scramble to go out on a call. Things can be chaotic. And what about former volunteers? One of them might have a key."

"But why would anyone want to hurt Tony?"

"We don't know that Tony was the target," Danny said. "We all use the ropes. Maybe whoever did this just wanted to hurt any one of us?"

She shivered. "Who would do something so terrible?"

"I don't know. Ex-spouse? Ex-lover? A former volunteer who washed out or was dismissed for some reason? Or maybe Tony really was the target—as captain, he might have felt responsible if someone was injured on his watch."

"He's only been captain a couple of years." The group elected its own officers by general consent. There was no definite schedule for changing office, but the members tended to rotate the various positions. Carrie had been second-in-command since last year, and she had accepted the role only after she had been reassured her primary function would be to assist Tony. The idea that she might have to step in to lead the group had seemed so remote it wasn't worth considering. "Maybe we should ask around and see what we can find out before we involve the police," she said.

Danny settled back into his seat. "When was the last time a SAR member had a bad accident like this?" he asked. "Do you remember?"

"Ryan and I were caught in that avalanche when we were training earlier this year." She still remembered the terror of a river of snow washing over her and pulling her under, though the others had found her and pulled her free within minutes. Ryan had escaped injury also, since the slide had been small. "And Ryan was badly hurt when Charlie Cutler pushed him off the side of Mount Baker." The convicted serial killer had been running from the police. She glanced at him. "Cutler tried to kill you, too, didn't he?"

Danny shrugged. "I got out of it with a few bruises and a sore knee. But, escaped serial killers aside, this kind of thing is really rare."

"It's kind of amazing, given the nature of the work we do," Carrie said. Personally, she tried not to think about the danger involved in rescuing people from remote wilderness, high mountains, deep canyons and rushing rivers. Better to focus on what a great service they were providing, and not personal risk.

"Barb and Cecil Kellogg slid off the road into the creek on a rescue call six years ago," Danny said. "Cecil broke his collarbone and Barb tore up her knee. They both left the team not long after that."

"This is different," she said. "Tony could have been killed if he had fallen from a great height."

"He might still not make it," Danny said. "We don't know what kind of internal injuries he might have, and all those injuries—sometimes the body can't cope."

"Don't say that. He's going to make it." She had depended on Tony so often, her role model for getting past those things about the search and rescue that threatened to overwhelm her.

They fell silent, an aching tension filling the car as they both contemplated their friend's possible fate. "How long have you been with search and rescue?" she asked as she turned onto the highway toward Junction, desperate to shift the conversation somewhere less dark.

"Seven years? Something like that. They put out a call for volunteers with medical experience and I thought it sounded pretty interesting."

"So a little longer than me," she said.

"I remember your first day," he said. "If I was a betting man, I would have said you wouldn't stick around. I guess I owe you an apology for that."

She hazarded a look at him. He wore an amused expression. "Why do you say that?" she asked.

"For one thing, most of our volunteers are climbers or have previous SAR experience, or have a medical or military background. They have a lot of outdoor experience."

"You make it sound like I was some couch potato who'd never been on a hike." She couldn't keep the huffiness from her voice. "I was trained in CPR and first aid and I'd been a life guard. I like hiking and I wanted to help people."

"I'm pretty sure you're the only member we've had who's a single mom with two little kids."

"What's that supposed to mean?"

He blew out a breath. "Don't get upset. I just mean the training we do, not to mention the actual calls, require a lot of time away from home. Seems like that would be hard with kids."

Was he implying that she neglected her children? "My kids understand search and rescue is important work. And I'm lucky enough to have my mom to help look after them."

"I get it," he said. "You're a great role model for them. Most people just aren't willing to make that sacrifice."

"It's not a sacrifice for me." When she had moved to Eagle Mountain following her divorce, she had been lost, wondering what to do with her life. She had a good job as an architect, but it wasn't enough. She felt helpless and was desperate for something that would make her feel stronger and more confident. When she saw a poster calling for recruits for the local search and rescue team it struck a chord in her. "I like challenging myself," she said. "And I like working with our team."

"You're good at it. I mean that."

"Why did you join SAR?" she asked. "I get that you thought it was interesting, but you've stayed all this time, so you must get more out of it than that."

"Like you said, it's a good team. And unlike you, I have a lot of free time—I work three twelve-hour shifts a week in a surgery unit and have the rest of the week to do what I want. In the winter I volunteer with backcountry ski patrol, but that's not very demanding. I have plenty of time for search and rescue. It's kind of addictive, you know?"

She nodded. She wasn't as much of an adrenaline junkie as some of her fellow volunteers, but she recognized the rush of taking big risks to save lives. When you succeeded, there was no other feeling like it.

"I didn't mean to insult you," he said again. "I admire you. I really do. And you've done a great job. I'm glad you stayed. And I'm not just saying that because you're in charge now." He grinned, a charming grin that sent a flutter through her stomach. That flutter surprised her so much she had to jerk her attention back to the road before she drifted onto the shoulder.

Danny was known for charming women, but he had certainly never charmed her. Her divorce had rendered her charm proof, she was sure.

Open mouth, insert foot, Danny thought as they neared Junction's city limits. He usually handled himself better with women. In his defense, he hadn't been trying to flirt with Carrie or anything. She was his fellow team member. Sure, she was an attractive woman, but she had made it clear from day one that she wasn't interested in anything but a professional relationship, and he tried to respect that. Just as well, since she probably thought he was an idiot now.

She parked her SUV in the hospital's garage and they made their way to the main entrance and approached the front desk. "We're trying to find out information about a patient here, Tony Meisner," Carrie said.

The woman behind the desk—gray hair, gray glasses, gray sweater—tapped out something on her keyboard and frowned at the computer screen. "Mr. Meisner is in ICU. Are you a relative?"

"We—" Danny began.

"I'm his sister," Carrie said.

The woman frowned. "Let me check his file."

She started typing again, and Danny took Carrie's

arm and pulled her toward the elevator bank. "Why does she have to check his file?" Carrie asked.

"She's probably seeing who is listed as next of kin." He checked the directory for ICU and hustled her inside an open car, where he pressed the button for the right floor, then the button to close the elevator doors. "The thing about hospitals is if you look like you know where you're supposed to be, most of the time they won't stop you," he said. "If I'd been thinking clearer, I'd have worn my scrubs."

"Have you worked at this hospital before?" she asked.

"No. I'm at a surgical center in Delta. But I doubt things are much different here." He led the way to the ICU, marching past the nurses' station, though a sideways glance told him it was unoccupied at the moment. The Intensive Care Unit was set up with rooms in a half circle, the patient's name clearly marked next to each door. Tony was midway through the circle, the door half-open.

He slipped into the room and Carrie followed, both of them moving as silently as possible. They stood at the end of the bed and stared. Tony, a tall, thin man, looked less tall and much thinner in the hospital gown, festooned with tubes and lines for IV, catheter, pulse oximeter, blood pressure, oxygen cannula and heart monitor. Beside him a screen traced a continuous EKG and registered his oxygen saturation and blood pressure readings. He wore casts on one arm and one leg and probably had other bandages they couldn't see under the blankets draped over him. His eyes were closed, sunken and shadowed in a face that looked gaunt and pallid.

Carrie covered her mouth with her hand but said nothing for a long while, then she straightened, removed her hand and murmured softly, "Tony? Are you awake?"

The door opened behind them and a woman in blue scrubs, dark curly hair pulled back in a bun, approached. "Hello?" she said, the question mark at the end of the single word leaving them to fill in the blank on the query.

"This is Tony's sister, Carrie." Danny stepped aside so the nurse could see her more clearly. "I'm her husband, Danny. I'm a nurse over at Delta."

Some—but not all—of the tension went out of the nurse's face. "Your brother has been out of surgery about thirty minutes," she said. "The doctor is keeping him heavily sedated."

"How is he doing?" Carrie asked. "I see the bandages, but what is the extent of his injuries?"

"We were with him when he fell," Danny said. It wouldn't hurt to let the woman know they were aware of the circumstances of the accident. "It was quite a shock."

"He was climbing?" the nurse asked.

"Rappelling into a canyon," Carrie said.

The nurse shook her head. "I don't know why these young men want to risk their lives like that."

Danny could have pointed out that Tony had been training to save lives, but he didn't bother. He couldn't be sure the woman at the front desk wouldn't decide to send security after them, so they shouldn't waste any time. "Can you tell us about his injuries?" he asked.

"Broken right leg—tibia and fibula. Several broken ribs. One of them punctured his lung on the way over here. Broken radius of the right arm. Various minor contusions and strains. He had surgery to pin some of the bones together and deal with the collapsed lung. He's stable, but still critical."

"Is there anything we can do?" Carrie asked. "Donate blood or something like that?"

"Nothing right now." The nurse checked Tony's IV. "Please limit your visit to five minutes. Even though he's sedated, he may be aware you're here. That's good, but we don't want to tax him."

Neither of them spoke after the nurse left. Danny tried to assess the situation as he would one of his patients at the hospital in Delta, but the knowledge that this was Tony—his friend—kept interfering. Besides, there was too much he didn't know, medically, to make any kind of accurate guess as to Tony's prognosis.

Carrie took a step back. "Let's get out of here," she said.

He followed her out of the room and back along the hallway to the elevator bank. When they were in the car alone, she turned to him. "Husband?" she asked.

"I wasn't sure they'd buy that I was a brother, but a sister's husband is close enough to be allowed into the ICU." He took out his phone. "I took a photo of the whiteboard in his room."

"Why?"

"It has the nurses' station's direct number." He showed her the image. "Now you can call and identify yourself as Tony's sister and get an update, bypassing the main switchboard. Give me your number and I'll forward it to you."

Her expression softened. Maybe she didn't think he was such an idiot after all. "Thanks."

"Can we grab dinner? And coffee?" Now that the rush of adrenaline following the accident had faded, he could use both.

"Just something fast." She checked her phone. "I really need to get home. My mom is great, but it's Saturday and I'd like to spend a little time with my kids."

"Sure."

They ate burgers and fries in the parking lot of a fast-food restaurant, with the SUV's heater running. Neither of them had been up to the brightly lit interior of the place, with half a dozen children racing about in the aftermath of a soccer game or something. "Tell me about your kids," he said.

She glanced at him. "Do you really want to know?"

"Yeah, I really want to know." He dunked a French fry in ketchup. "I like children."

"Dylan is nine and Amber is eight." Something like a smile softened her face. "They're great kids. I know every parents says that, but they are. Smart and kind and just...great."

"You must have had them pretty young." He had pegged her as being pretty close to his own age, which was thirty.

"I was nineteen when Dylan was born, and I had

Amber thirteen months later." She met his questioning gaze. "I married my ex a month after we graduated high school."

"Wow. I didn't know people still did that."

"Yeah, wow."

"So, how long have you been divorced? Or is that too nosy?"

"Six and a half years. I found out he was cheating while I was pregnant with Amber."

"Ouch."

"People tried to warn us. Or they tried to warn me, at least. We were too young. He wasn't ready to settle down. But my mom was only eighteen when she had me. She was seventeen when she married my dad—he was twenty. And they were happy together for twenty years until he was killed by a drunk driver."

"I'm sorry for your loss."

"Thanks. I think with my ex and me, it wasn't really immaturity that killed our marriage, it was the fact that he really didn't want to be married."

"Do you still see him?"

"Occasionally. He drops in and out of the kids' life, which drives me crazy, but they seem resilient, and at least I'm not relying on him for support. I'd be out of luck if I was."

He heard the bitterness behind her words, but who could blame her?

"What about you?" she asked. "Have you ever been married?"

"No way."

She laughed. "Well, tell me how you really feel."

He dug around in the paper bag, searching for more fries. “I don’t think I’m marriage material.”

“Well, if you think that, it’s probably a good idea not to get married.” She turned the key in the ignition. “You ready to head back?”

He was, and they did. They didn’t say much on the way home, and he found himself watching her in the fading light. She really was pretty—honey-blond hair past her shoulder blades, strands coming loose from the braid she wore today. She was fit—that was a given for search and rescue. Doing the math, he knew she was only twenty-eight or twenty-nine, but she had an air of maturity about her. Maybe having kids did that. He knew she worked as an architect—her name was on the plaque at an office just off Main of a firm that designed high-end houses. The only woman on that list, he remembered. Did that feel odd to her, or did she even care?

He thought of himself as being good at reading people, but he had never been able to read Carrie. He didn’t like to admit how much that bothered him, but there it was. She kept herself to herself, much like he did. People thought of him as outgoing, but that was just another way of keeping them from getting too close.

They saw the flashing lights as they climbed the hill toward search and rescue headquarters. Red-and-blue strobes bathed the snowbanks around the building in a kaleidoscope of light and shadow. Two fire trucks and two sheriff’s department vehicles filled the lot, along with several cars he recognized as belonging to fellow SAR volunteers. "What is going on?" Carrie asked, fear tightening her voice.

Sheri trotted up to meet them, her husband, Colorado State Patrol detective Erik Lester, close behind. Carrie stopped the SUV and lowered her window. Icy air rushed in, along with the smell of smoke and hot metal. "What happened?" she asked.

"The Beast is gone," Sheri said. "Burned up." She glanced over her shoulder at what Danny could now see was the blackened hull of a vehicle. "I hated that old thing most of the time, but what are we going to do without it?"

The Beast had been the primary transportation for SAR volunteers and gear. Ancient and outdated, it was still the best thing they had for those purposes, and the organization—always strapped for cash—had never had the money to replace it.

Erik nudged Sheri aside so he could address Carrie. "I understand you're in charge, with Tony in the hospital."

"How is Tony?" Sheri asked before Carrie could reply to Erik.

"He was out of surgery and critical but stable," Carrie said. "He's in intensive care."

"He was sedated, so we didn't get to talk to him," Danny added.

Carrie turned to Erik. "Do you need me to sign papers or something?"

"I need to ask if you know of anyone who might have a grudge against search and rescue or someone in the group." Erik said.

"I don't understand," Carrie said. "What does that have to do with this fire?" She looked toward the charred remains of the Beast.

"We don't think this fire was an accident," Erik said. "We're pretty sure someone torched the Beast deliberately."

Chapter Three

Carrie tried to comprehend this statement, but the words floated on the surface, refusing to sink in or have meaning. "Are you talking arson?" Danny asked. "Someone deliberately torched the Beast?"

Erik nodded. "We'll know more after the investigator's final report, but everything points to that right now."

"I told him about Tony," Sheri said. "How his fall might not have been an accident."

"Sheri said you suspected chemical damage to Tony's climbing ropes," Erik said.

"Yes." Carrie finally found her voice.

Sheriff Travis Walker, his tall, broad-shouldered silhouette recognizable even in the darkness, strode toward them. He nodded to Carrie. "Where was the search and rescue vehicle parked when you last saw it?" he asked.

"Right next to the building." She looked toward SAR headquarters, dark and silent. And unharmed. "There's a designated parking spot for the Beast right by the door," she said. "How did the Jeep burn and the building isn't touched?"

Travis and Erik exchanged looks. "The Jeep was parked up by the road when it burned," Travis said. "Between a snowbank and the asphalt. Nothing else impacted."

"Who has the keys to the vehicle?" Erik asked.

"They're kept on a hook just inside the door of the headquarters," Sheri said. "Anyone could access them."

"Anyone with a key to the building," Carrie said.

"And who is that?" Travis asked.

"Any member of search and rescue," Danny said. "Probably some former members, too."

Travis's frown told Carrie what he thought of such lax security. "We have to be able to respond to an emergency at any time," she said. "Whoever reports here first starts loading up the gear we'll need." It was a process that had worked well for over thirty years.

"I want to take a look at the ropes Tony was using when he fell," Travis said.

"Do you really think there's a connection between the Beast being destroyed and what happened to Tony?" Even as Carrie asked the question, she realized how desperate she sounded. The SAR captain had almost been killed this morning, and the only vehicle the organization owned had been destroyed tonight. What else could they think but that someone was trying to harm Eagle Mountain Search and Rescue?

She unlocked the side door to the building and flipped on the lights, flooding the large concrete-floored expanse with a harsh white glow. "Does anything look out of place?" Erik asked.

She scanned the area. Gear hung on hooks and was stored in bins along the back wall, and long tables at the front of the room held a couple of coffee cups, some recruiting brochures and a box of nitrile gloves someone had forgotten to stow. A sagging sofa and an assortment of folding chairs occupied most of the rest of the space. The air smelled of coffee, disinfectant and the lingering odor of the pizza they had ordered in a couple of days before. "Everything looks fine," she said. The very ordinariness of it chilled her, considering what had happened.

"Where are the climbing ropes?" Travis asked.

"Over here." Danny led the way to the table where the broken climbing ropes were laid out. "You can see where the fibers disintegrated," he said, pointing to the place where the strands had separated. "And there's discoloration around the breaks. It's hard to see, but if you take a whiff, you can smell some kind of acid."

Travis bent close to the ropes and sniffed, then nodded. He looked up at Erik. "Can you have the state lab test this for us?"

"Sure thing. I'll get an evidence bag from my car." He left, and Travis moved away from the table.

"Who might have tampered with the ropes?" Travis asked.

"All the search and rescue team members know where the gear is stored and would have access to it." Her stomach knotted as the implication of that sank in. Of course they had talked about one of the other volunteers being responsible, but having law enforcement reach the same conclusion made it seem more real. She trusted her fellow volunteers with her life. They were a team. Who would betray them this way?

"Someone else could have come in and done it," Danny said. "People monitor the emergency channel. They would know when we were out on a call."

"We're supposed to lock up every time we leave, but maybe someone was careless," Sheri said.

"What about the Beast?" Carrie asked. "Why do you think that was arson and not just, I don't know, something wrong with the engine? We're always having problems with it."

"We'll have a full report in a couple of days, but the fire crew that responded said they could smell diesel and it looked like someone soaked the area around the vehicle and tossed in a match," Travis said. "It went up like a bomb."

She wrapped her arms around herself, cold to the bone despite the murmur of the building's furnace.

Erik returned and collected the severed ropes. Sheri left with him, and the sheriff followed them out. Danny put a hand on Carrie's shoulder. "Are you okay?"

Just like that, she was hyperaware of him again, of his quiet strength and the warmth in both his hand and his voice seeping into her. It would be so easy to lean into him, to imagine some connection between them that entitled her to take comfort from him.

Instead, she uncrossed her arms and straightened. "I'm fine. It's just a shock, something like this."

"Yeah. You should go home," he said.

"I will. You too."

"Yeah."

They walked out together and she made a point of locking the door and trying the knob to make sure it was secure. Danny waved, then drove off in his car, and she followed him down the hill and into town. Foot traffic on the sidewalks had died down and only a couple of restaurants and Mo's Pub showed signs of life. She turned off Main Street and drove to the small house she shared with her mom.

"I heard fire engines go by an hour ago," her mother, Becky, said when she met Carrie at the door. Not yet fifty, Becky was petite like her daughter, with naturally frosted blond hair cut in a chin-length bob. "I was afraid you had to go out on another search and rescue call."

"I would have phoned you if I had." Carrie hung up her coat and dropped her purse and keys on the end of the counter. "Are the kids in bed?"

"They went sledding with Ruthie and Evan Morris this afternoon and were tired out," Becky said.

Carrie tiptoed down the hallway and peeked into the first room on the left. Dylan lay on his back, one hand thrown across his chest, one leg out of the covers, blond hair fallen across his forehead. At peace. Smiling, she moved to the door across from his, where Amber lay curled on her side beneath her pink quilt, her princess night-light bathing the room in a muted pink glow.

Back in the kitchen, her mother switched on the

electric kettle. “I thought I’d make some tea,” Becky said. “Do you want some?”

“Yes.” Carrie sank into a chair at the table, exhaustion pulling at her like lead weights.

“How is Tony?” Becky asked. “Were you able to see him?”

“He was out of surgery and I saw him, but he’s sedated. His condition is listed as stable but critical.”

“Did you have anything to eat? I could warm up some soup.”

“We stopped for a burger on the way home. Thanks.”

“Someone went with you. I’m glad to hear it.” Becky dropped tea bags into cups and took out a jar of sugar. “Who was it?”

“Danny Irwin. He was climbing alongside Tony when Tony fell. I think it probably shook him up a lot.” Danny hadn’t shown any outward signs of distress, but there had been real concern beneath his calm, and his normally jovial manner had been more subdued.

“I hope Tony gets better.” Becky poured water over the tea bags. “I don’t know him as well as you do, but he’s always struck me as a really nice man.”

“He is,” Carrie said.

“Do they have any idea how the fall happened?” Becky brought two mugs to the table and slid one toward Carrie. The scent of mint perfumed the air. Chamomile-and-mint tea, her mother’s solution to every worry.

“We’re not sure.” That was all she had intended to say, but the rest came rushing out. “But it might have been deliberate. The sheriff took the ropes Tony was using to be tested. Danny thinks someone might have poured some kind of acid on them. The damage wasn't really evident, but the ropes failed and Tony fell."

"That's horrible! Who would do something like that?" Becky's voice rose and Carrie cast a worried glance toward the hallway and the children's rooms.

Becky leaned forward and lowered her voice. "Seriously, does anyone know who would do something like that to Tony?"

"No idea." Carrie sipped her tea. She really didn't want to say anything else, but Eagle Mountain was too small a town for her mother not to find out about the Beast as soon as she reported to the courthouse Monday morning for her job with the county clerk's office. "Those fire engines you heard earlier were responding to a fire at search and rescue headquarters," she said. "Someone set fire to the Beast."

Becky's eyes widened. "You're kidding. Why would someone target search and rescue? You help people."

"I wish I was kidding. I know the old thing was a pain in the butt sometimes, but now we'll have to replace it and we really don't have the money."

"You'll have to hold a fundraiser or two," Becky said. "People will want to contribute.'

Carrie nodded and pushed aside her cup. "I'm beat. I'm going to take a shower and crawl into bed."

"Sleep well," Becky said.

But Carrie knew that wasn't going to happen. Not tonight, and maybe not for a long time to come.

DANNY WOKE TO find a wet spring snow beginning to fall but wasn't surprised when he received a text from Carrie calling a special meeting at search and rescue headquarters. Better to get everyone together to talk about this now, on Sunday when most people would have the day off and be able to attend. He usually spent his Sundays working ski patrol in one of the popular backcountry areas around town, but after yesterday's ordeal he had sent a text to the volunteer coordinator begging off. He had planned to spend the day sleeping and watching TV—a whole day to himself, when no one needed him.

But he wouldn't pass up the opportunity to hear the latest news and speculations about Tony's accident or the destruction of the Beast.

Shortly before he had to leave for the meeting, his phone rang. The familiar mixture of panic and dread filled him as he stared at the caller ID. He sucked in a breath and answered. "Hey, Joy. How are you?"

"Not so good." His sister sounded as if she hadn't slept in a while, his first clue she wasn't just calling to complain or ask for money. "Mom isn't doing so well," she said. "She's been talking about how she doesn't need to take her medicine anymore. The way she's been acting, I'm wondering if she's already stopped taking her prescription."

"You keep track of the pills, right?" Danny asked.

"Yes, but maybe she's throwing them away when I'm not looking. You know how devious she can be."

Their mother was smart, which sometimes worked against her.

"Something's not right," Joy said. "After all this time, I can tell."

"I'll talk to her," Danny said. Sometimes, he could reason with Mom and take some of the load off Joy.

"Call tonight. She left this morning. She said she was going out with friends, but she doesn't really have friends, so I don't know where she is. And she never answers her phone when she's gone like this."

"I'll call tonight," he said, the familiar fear twisting his stomach in a knot. "Have you talked to her doctor?"

"Of course. He says he can authorize inpatient treatment for a little while, if Mom will agree to go."

A big *if.* "I'll talk to her," he said again.

"Great. I'm going to lie down now." *Click.*

Danny signed. Joy was probably depressed. Caring for their ill—and uncooperative—mother was taking its toll. But what else were they going to do? His mother and sister lived in Iowa. Danny's life was here in Colorado. Their mother refused any other assistance. And much of the time she refused to help herself. They were all doing the best they could, but he had stopped pretending it was enough.

He set a reminder in his phone to call later and headed to the SAR meeting. He wasn't surprised to find the parking lot already full of cars when he arrived shortly before noon. It looked like everyone who had even a peripheral role with the team had shown up. Like Danny, they were probably hoping for an update about both Tony and the Beast.

"Thank you for coming on such short notice," Carrie said from the front of the room. Every chair and the sofa was filled with volunteers, and several people, including Danny, stood along the walls. "I know you're all worried about Tony. I spoke with the hospital a little while ago and he's awake and they've even had him up and moving about a little. He's still in critical condition and can't have visitors, and he's in a lot of pain, but we know he's tough."

"Tell him I said he's too mean to die," Ryan said, and received a few laughs.

"Where's Austen?" Eldon asked. "Why isn't he here?"

"I had a text saying he'd be here." Carrie frowned. "It's not like him to be late." As the newest member of the team, still in his training program, Austen had been more dedicated than most, showing up for every call and every training session.

"Ted isn't here, either," Sheri said. "But don't wait for them. Have the police discovered anything about the damage to Tony's harness or the fire that destroyed the Jeep?"

"I called the sheriff, but I haven't heard anything," Carrie said. "He indicated last night that it could take several days to get results from the state lab on the climbing ropes Tony was using, and from the arson investigator."

"Why destroy the Beast?" Eldon asked. "Does someone seriously not want us to be able to go out on rescue calls?"

"I've wanted to torch the old clunker plenty of

times myself," Danny said. "But I would have waited until we had a replacement to do it."

"Even if they find the lowlife who set the fire, we've still lost our only response vehicle," Sheri said. "What are we going to do now?"

"We'll have to use our personal vehicles," Carrie said. "I filed a claim with our insurance carrier this morning, but we're only going to be able to collect a couple of thousand dollars at most. The Beast wasn't worth that much to anyone but us."

The door opened, letting in a blast of cold air, and Ted stamped inside. He brushed snow from the shoulders of his jacket. "Sorry I'm late," he said. "It's snowing hard out there." He hung up the jacket and joined the others. "What did I miss?"

"We were just talking about the Beast," Sheri said.

"We'll have to find a replacement," Ted said.

"The Beast was specially modified for search and rescue work," Danny said. "Getting something to replace it is going to run upwards of a hundred K."

"We'll need to raise money," Carrie said. "I want a couple of people to work on a contribution plea to send out to donors who have supported us in the past, and to come up with ideas for other fundraisers."

Silence met this announcement, as the volunteers avoided looking at each other. "I'll volunteer," Sheri said finally. "Eldon, you can work with me."

"Sure," Eldon said.

"Thank you." Carrie glanced down at the tablet on which she had apparently scribbled some notes. "The sheriff asked me to compile a list of everyone who has a key to the headquarters building. I'll need help figuring out who—besides those of us in this room—might have access." She looked across the room. "Ted, I'm hoping you'll help me with that. You've been a member longer than anyone else."

"I don't see the point," Ted said. "It wasn't a search and rescue volunteer who did this. The older members know how hard we worked to get the Beast in the first place. We held spaghetti suppers, car washes, silent auctions, sold T-shirts. We worked our tails off to pay for the thing. And the newer volunteers know how much we relied on the Beast to get us and our gear to accident sites in the mountains. I've known every volunteer with search and rescue for the past thirty years and none of them would do this."

"Maybe it wasn't a volunteer," Danny said. "Maybe it was a friend or family member of a volunteer who resented the organization taking up their time."

"Or just a nutcase who decided it would be fun to set something on fire," Eldon said.

"What happened to Tony wasn't a spur-of-the-moment decision," Sheri said. "Someone planned to ruin his ropes and put him in danger."

"Whoever did it ought to be charged with attempted murder," Eldon said.

Everyone started talking at once, voices rising with anger and outrage. Carrie let them talk but said nothing. Danny was silent, too, watching her. She looked so calm, only a tightness around her eyes and mouth betraying her concern. They were lucky to have her to assume command in Tony's absence. He had never thought of her as a leader before, but she was exactly the person they needed right now.

"Ted, I want a list of all the people who have worked with search and rescue so far," she said when the conversation had died to a murmur. "Danny, I want you to make a list of everyone in Tony's life—friends, relatives, people at his job. I want to know everyone who might have had a grudge against him or against SAR."

"Okay, but why me?" he asked.

"You know Tony as well as anyone. And since you're a nurse, you can get in to see him in ICU and ask him if he has any idea who did this."

"Maybe we should leave all this 'making lists' and questioning people to the cops," Eldon said. "I mean, that's their job."

"And I'm sure they're going to investigate," Carrie said. "But I want to do whatever we can to help them. Tony is one of our own. I want him to know we're doing our part to stop whoever damaged those ropes and to keep them from hurting someone else."

"Did the same person damage the ropes and set fire to the Beast?" Sheri asked.

"We don't know," Carrie said. "But I'm curious to see if any names show up on our lists of people with a key to headquarters and people who interacted regularly with Tony."

"Every one of us will be on both lists," Eldon said.

Silence. They had probably all been thinking the same thing, but having it said out loud—that the saboteur was one of them—was too terrible.

"The cops are going to look at all of us first," Danny

said. “We might as well be ready for that. And if we can find someone else we think they should look at instead, then we need to do it.”

The door to the outside burst open and banged against the wall. They turned as Austen Morrissey staggered inside. Blood ran from a gash on his head and his clothes were wet, his pants legs smeared with mud. “Austen! What happened to you?” Sheri rushed forward and took his arm.

“I was on the way here and someone ran my car off the road.” He sank into a chair and looked up at them, eyes wide. “They came straight at me. I ran into the ditch. I guess I hit my head.” He touched the gash and winced. “I must have blacked out for a little bit. I managed to get out of the car and hike up the road, but I’m a mess. I mean, it’s crazy, but I think somebody tried to kill me.”

Chapter Four

Blood ran down Austen's face and stained his light gray jacket. "Sit down and let me take a look at you," Danny said. He took Austen by the elbow and guided him to a folding chair.

"Should I call an ambulance?" Carrie asked.

"No! I'll be fine." Austen tried to stand, but Danny gently pushed him back into the chair.

Danny checked Austen's pupils, which looked normal. He guessed Austen was in his early thirties, with a broad face, wide-set blue eyes and a dusting of freckles, which combined to make him look young and guileless. "Let's get some of this blood cleaned up and see what we're dealing with," Danny said. "You might need stitches."

Carrie brought him a bottle of saline and a packet of gauze pads, and Danny used these to clean the blood from what turned out to be a fairly shallow gash just above Austen's right eyebrow. "This doesn't look too bad," Danny said. "Head wounds always bleed a lot, and you've got a good-sized lump. How many fingers am I holding up?"

"Three," Austen said. "Honestly, I'm fine—just shook up."

"What happened?" Ted asked. He and the others had gathered around.

Austen gripped his knees, his knuckles white as Danny dabbed antiseptic on the wound, but he didn't flinch. "It was snowing pretty hard, so I didn't see much," he said. "I was headed up the big hill toward headquarters and I saw the headlights of a vehicle coming toward me. They were superbright, and I flashed my lights at the driver to remind him to dim them, but instead, they kept coming right toward me. By the time I realized he was in my lane and he wasn't slowing down, all I could do was steer toward the ditch. I banged my head when I went off the road."

"You say the driver was a man?" Carrie asked.

"I don't know." Austen touched the lump on his head and winced. "The car's headlights were blinding me. I can't even tell you what kind of vehicle it was."

"Where is your car?" Danny asked.

"I left it in the ditch and walked up here." He looked down at his boots, the leather dark with dampness. "I guess that was a dumb thing to do."

"We should call the sheriff," Carrie said. She pulled her phone from her pocket.

"They're not going to be able to do anything," Austen said. "I can't tell them much."

"Maybe they'll find something," Carrie said. "And if nothing else, I want this on record."

While Carrie moved away to speak to the 9-1-1

operator, Danny finished bandaging Austen. "Any other injuries?" he asked when he was done.

"Only to my pride," Austen said.

"A deputy is on his way." Carrie rejoined them. "How are you doing, Austen?"

"I'm okay." He continued to stare at his shoes.

Carrie put a hand on his shoulder. "I imagine this was pretty upsetting, after the accident you were in a couple of years ago."

Austen's mouth tightened. "Yeah, it was a bit of déjà vu."

Danny sent Carrie a questioning look. What was she talking about?

She shook her head. *Later*, she mouthed.

"Austen, I've got my truck with me," Eldon said. "Maybe I can pull your car out of the ditch once the deputy has had a look."

Austen looked up and seemed to gather himself together. "Thanks," he said. "I'd really appreciate that." He looked around. "Do we have any coffee?"

"I'll get you a cup," Sheri said.

The others talked among themselves and to Austen as Danny packed up the first aid supplies. Carrie met him at the medical closet. "I don't think Austen should be driving," she said. "Would you mind taking him home? He can worry about the car tomorrow."

"Sure. What was that about him having been through something like this before?"

"Don't you remember?" She glanced over her shoulder toward Austen, who was surrounded by the others, deep in conversation. Carrie looked back at

Danny. "Summer, two years ago? He and his girlfriend—she may have been his fiancée, I don't remember—were in a horrible accident on Briar Patch Road. The Jeep they were in slipped off the road and rolled in Poughkeepsie Canyon. Austen was thrown clear near the top and only suffered a broken shoulder, but his girlfriend was seriously injured. They had to airlift her out of the canyon. She was alive when we got to her, but she didn't make it."

"I heard something about that," Danny said. "But I was away for almost a month that summer, dealing with family stuff." His mother had been struggling through a particularly bad period back then. He glanced back at Austen. "Was he living here then?"

"No. They were on vacation from Texas or Arizona or someplace like that. He moved here later. He said he was so inspired by the work search and rescue did that he wanted to be a part of that."

"No wonder what happened today shook him up so much."

She nodded. "I'll feel better if I know someone is seeing him home safely—someone with medical experience, in case that knock on the head was worse than it seems."

The door from the outside opened again, bringing in a swirl of snow and Rayford County sheriff's deputy—and new SAR recruit—Jake Gwynn. He surveyed the room, then focused on Austen's bandaged head. "I understand there's been some trouble," he said.

"Someone ran my car off the road," Austen said. "But before you ask, I didn't see who it was."

Jake pulled up an empty folding chair and sat in front of Austen. "Start at the beginning and tell me everything that happened."

Austen told the same story he had shared with them and wasn't able to provide more details, despite Jake's questions. When he was done, Jake tucked his notebook back into his pocket. "I'll stop and take a look at your car on my way back into town," he said. "But it's snowing hard enough it's probably already obliterated any tread patterns from the other vehicle."

"I told Carrie she shouldn't even bother to call you," Austen said. "I'm sorry we got you out on such a nasty day."

"I called because I wanted this on record," Carrie said. "Jake, you know about the other attacks on search and rescue?"

Jake nodded. "I know about the damage to Tony's climbing ropes and the burning of the SAR Jeep. Have there been others?"

"Not until this attack on Austen," she said.

"What makes you think this accident is related to those other incidents?" Jake asked.

"Austen told you this other vehicle headed straight toward him, with its bright lights on," Carrie said. "Who has their bright lights on in the middle of the day, even if it is snowing? It wasn't an accident, it was a deliberate attempt to harm one of our members."

"It could have been a drunk driver," Jake said. "Or even someone who didn't see Austen in the snowstorm until it was too late. How would this other driver have even known who Austen was and that he's a member of search and rescue?"

"There are no other homes and businesses up this road," Danny said. "Anyone driving up here was most likely with SAR."

"For all we know, whoever is doing this knows all about us," Sheri said. "From what kind of car we drive and where we live to whether or not we have a partner waiting at home."

"It's a pretty tenuous connection," Jake said. "I'll do what I can, but we don't have much to go on."

"What about the sabotaged climbing ropes and the burned-out Jeep?" Eldon asked. "Do you have any clues as to who is responsible for those?"

"No." Jake looked around at them. Their faces reflected anger, worry, annoyance or a combination of all three emotions. "Can you think of anyone who might have a grudge against search and rescue?" he asked. "Someone you angered or maybe the relative of someone you weren't able to save."

"Most people are grateful that we try to save their loved ones," Ted said. "Even when our job is to retrieve a body from a remote location, the families are relieved to have that closure."

Jake nodded. "Keep thinking. And we'll keep looking for clues. In the meantime, everyone be careful."

He left and Austen stood. "Let's see about my car, okay Eldon?" he said.

"The car can wait until morning," Danny said. "The cops probably aren't finished with it yet anyway. I'll take you home."

Austen hesitated. “I don’t know…”

“Let Danny take you home,” Carrie said. “You probably shouldn’t be driving right now anyway.”

Austen nodded. “I guess you’re right. Thanks, Danny.”

Austen followed Danny to his car, a battered green Honda that had seen better days but served him well. He followed Austen’s directions to a new set of condos on the outskirts of town, built as part of an affordable-housing initiative. “What do you do for work?” Danny asked. “I don’t think I ever heard.”

“I’m the manager for these condos,” Austen said.

“What led you to join SAR?” Danny asked. Though Carrie had told him the story, he was curious to hear what Austen would say. “We recruit heavily in the climbing community and among medical personnel like me, but I’m always curious what brings others to the group.”

“Eagle Mountain Search and Rescue saved my life,” Austen said. “A couple of years ago I was in a bad accident in Poughkeepsie Canyon. I thought you knew.”

“I was out of town a lot that year,” Danny said. “Family stuff. I guess I wasn’t here for that call. Looks like you made a full recovery.” No mention of the girlfriend, but maybe that was too painful to talk about.

“Yeah, but I figured the SAR training would help me get in better shape, and it has.” He unbuckled his seat belt. “You want to come in? I’m going to make more coffee.”

“Thanks. Coffee would be good.” He was curious

to know more about this rookie he hadn't interacted with all that much.

Austen unlocked the front door and led the way into a small foyer that opened into a combination living/dining room, with a galley kitchen along the back wall. "Make yourself comfortable," he said. "I'll get the coffee."

While Austen fiddled with a coffee-pod machine, Danny studied the simply furnished room. Where his own place was cluttered and messy, Austen's condo had the look of a hotel suite or a real estate show home. The furniture had the same neutral colors and clean lines that blended into the white walls and light wood flooring. There were no books or art. The only ornament at all was a photograph in a silver frame on a table by the sofa.

Danny studied the image of a smiling woman with brown curly hair, a slight gap between her upper front teeth.

"That's Julie, my fiancée." Austen spoke from right behind him.

Danny flinched and turned around. "I didn't mean to be nosy.

"It's okay." Austen set two mugs on the coffee table. "She died before I moved here. That's one of the reasons I came to Eagle Mountain. I wanted to make a fresh start."

He sat on one end of the sofa and Danny took the other and sipped from his coffee, trying to think of a suitable reply. "That must have been hard," he said after a moment.

"It was," Austen had a tightness around the mouth again, as if he was reining in emotion.

"I'm off tomorrow," Danny said. "I could pick you up and take you out to your car."

"Thanks, but I think I'll just call O'Brien's for a wrecker." He forced a smile. "That's what insurance is for, right? I guess I was so shaken earlier, I didn't think of it. I should have called them right away, come home and cleaned myself up and not said anything."

"No, you did the right thing, coming to the meeting. We need to know about this stuff."

Austen grimaced. "You heard the deputy—he thinks it was just a careless driver. But I know that car was headed straight for me." He set his mug on the coffee table and leaned forward, his elbows on his knees. "I wish I could figure out who wants to hurt us—to hurt search and rescue."

"Maybe it's like Jake said—someone has a grudge. Maybe someone who didn't make the cut to join the group."

"Does that happen very often?" Austen asked. "You kick people out?"

"Not everyone can meet the rigors of training or keep up with the demands on their time," Danny said. The coffee was already lukewarm, so he set the half-full cup aside. "And occasionally we get people who are so set on being heroes that they can't work as a team. The one thing you have to accept to do this kind of work is that it really isn't about you—it's about the community, the team and the people we're trying to help."

"I still struggle sometimes when people get into trouble because they did something stupid and we have to go out and save them," Austen said.

"Yeah, that can be annoying, but you learn to put that aside. You're doing a good job. I can see how you've improved in your training."

Austen straightened. "Thanks. That means a lot."

Danny stood. "I know you're probably worn out. I won't keep you. Thanks for the coffee."

"Thank you for the ride home." Austen walked with him to the door. "I guess SAR is kind of my family now," he said. "All these attacks feel personal."

"Yeah, it feels that way to me, too," Danny said.

"I want to find out who's doing this," Austen said. "And I want to stop them."

"We all want that," Danny said. "Maybe we'll think of something that can help the sheriff."

"If I figure out who this is, I'm not going to wait for the sheriff." His gaze met Danny's, the anger in them sharp and bright. "I'm going to make sure they never hurt anyone again."

"I WORRY ABOUT you taking on too much, stepping in as SAR captain in addition to everything else you have going on." Becky sat across the kitchen table from Carrie and regarded her daughter with a look of concern Carrie had seen so often it was the expression she most associated with her mom—a slight furrowing of the forehead, a narrowing of her eyes, lips pressed together in a way that deepened the lines on each side of her mouth. She had been startled, after her children were born, to recognize an identical expression on her own face at times.

"It's okay, Mom." Carrie pushed aside the stack of incident reports, training schedules and inventory sheets she had been studying. Though she had helped Tony with some of the paperwork a few times, the sheer volume of record keeping involved in running one rural, search and rescue operation had surprised her. "You know I like to keep busy," she said, and smiled in a way she hoped was reassuring.

"Sometimes, staying busy is a good way to avoid thinking about the rest of your life," Becky said.

Ouch. "What's that supposed to mean? My life is the kids and you, my job, and search and rescue. All things I love."

"What about your personal life?" Becky asked. "You're still a young woman. You should be dating."

"Says the woman who hasn't been on a date in how long is it now, ten years?"

"I'm not twenty-nine. You are." A flush stained Becky's cheeks, making her look even younger than her forty-eight years. "And my situation is different. No one could replace your father."

Carrie wanted to reassure her mother that she didn't have to replace Dad, but she didn't have to spend the rest of her life alone, either. But that would open the door for her mom to turn Carrie's words back on herself, and she didn't have the energy for that argument this evening.

But her mom wasn't going to drop the subject. "You live in a town where the men outnumber the women two to one, or something like that," she continued. "And they're all skiers and climbers and runners and outdoor guides. You could have your pick of sexy, fit men."

"Why would I want a guy who spends all his spare time climbing rocks or riding mountain bikes?" Carrie asked. "And why are you bringing this up now, Mom? What's happened to make you suddenly concerned about my single status?"

Becky's lips thinned and the lines on either side of her mouth deepened even more. "I overheard Amber talking with her friend, Kiley, today when we were all walking home from school. Kiley asked where Amber's daddy was and why didn't he live with them, and Amber said her dad didn't live with them because Mommy didn't want a daddy around, so she guessed that meant she'd never have one."

It wasn't the first time something one of her children said made Carrie feel like she'd swallowed rocks, but the sensation wasn't easier to take, no matter how much practice she had. "Don't you think having different men move in and out of my life while I tried to find 'the one' would be a lot harder on the children than leaving all that until they're older?" she asked.

"I think children are resilient and you can't be afraid to let someone into your heart because of what might happen." Becky caught and held Carrie's gaze. "I didn't raise a coward, Carrie Ann."

The words stung. "I am not a coward. Even when I hate something, like heights, I do exactly what you taught me—buck up and get on with it."

"You're the bravest person I know when it comes to saving other people's lives," Becky said. She reached across the table and squeezed Carrie's hand. "If it helps, think of relationships as another challenge to be overcome, like climbing a peak or rappelling into a canyon, only this time the person you're saving is yourself."

Carrie searched for some sharp reply to this remarkable statement but drew a blank. She was still struggling to find words when the doorbell rang.

Becky released Carrie's hand and checked the time on the microwave. "It's after seven. Were you expecting someone?"

"No." Carrie stood and hurried to the door as the bell rang again. She flipped the switch for the porch light and checked the security peep, and was surprised to see Ted staring back at her.

"Ted! Is something wrong? Did I miss a callout?" Dispatch was supposed to automatically send her a call and a text in case of emergency, but maybe something had gone wrong.

"Nothing like that." Ted shoved both hands in the pockets of his blue Eagle Mountain Search and Rescue parka. "Can I come in and talk to you about something?"

"Of course." She stepped back and let him pass into the living room. He was a tall man, a little hunched now, and he carried himself like someone who had probably taken up more space at one time. She wondered if he had played football when he was young. He had the frame for it, if not the weight.

He pulled off the green fleece hat he had been wearing and ran one hand through his still-thick white hair, which did nothing to neaten it. "I'm not interrupting your dinner or anything, am I?"

"No. Come on into the living room." She flipped on the light as she entered the small room with the sofa that turned into a bed, mostly used when her aunt Dorothy came to visit from Phoenix. "What did you want to talk about?" she asked.

He looked around the room, at everything in it but her. "Any news about Tony?" he asked.

"He was moved out of ICU into a regular room today," she said. "I'm going to see him tomorrow."

Ted nodded. "That's good. I remember when he joined search and rescue. He was just eighteen, the youngest member we'd had until then. This skinny kid who didn't know anything—had to learn everything from scratch. But he stuck with it. Terrible, that rope being damaged like that."

"Do you know something about what happened?" she asked. "Is that why you're here?"

He looked up, startled, as if he had only just remembered she was in the room. "No. I wanted to talk to you about the way I'm being sidelined with the group," he said. "I've got more experience than anyone on the squad, but because I'm older, I'm being skipped over for leadership roles and asked to take a secondary role on rescue missions. It isn't right."

The complaint didn't surprise her, but the force of the anger behind it did. "Let's sit down," she said, and motioned him to sit beside her on the sofa. He did so, perched on the edge of the cushion, as if prepared to spring up at any second. “We all respect your experience with search and rescue,” she began. “You’ve been a mentor to so many of us.”

“I’m not a mentor. I’m a fellow team member,” he said. “An active member, not a consultant, but that’s what Tony has been trying to make me, and I won’t stand for it.”

“I don’t think Tony has been doing that,” she said.

“I wanted to be the training officer this year,” he said. “It’s a job I’ve done before. I’ve done all the jobs before, but I’m especially good at that one. It’s like you said, I’m good at teaching others—mentoring them. But Tony gave the position to Sheri instead. He said she’s a stronger climber and that’s something we all need to work on more. Just because I messed up tying a knot one time, he’s never going to let me forget it.”

Carrie remembered the incident he was referring to. Ted had started down a rappel before he secured the end of his rope with a stopper knot so it would slide through the anchor chain when it reached the end. It was the kind of careless mistake that could cost a climber his life. Tony had seen what was happening and stopped Ted before he met with disaster. How ironic that Tony had been injured when his ropes slipped through the anchor, though in his case it had been no accident.

There hadn’t been any other missteps by Ted that Carrie was aware of, but even she had noticed that Ted was the slowest of the squad now, lagging behind on long hikes and tiring more quickly under duress. "Ted, you've been doing this kind of work a long time," she said.

"Almost thirty years," he said. "Longer than you've been alive."

She nodded. "Your body has taken a lot of beating in that time," she said. "Long hours, tough hikes, lots of nasty weather."

"It's part of the job. I don't complain."

"I guess what I'm trying to say is, it's normal that at some point you have to slow down. Your body is forcing you to, whether you want to or not."

"I'm not slowing down!" He jumped up and glared at her. "That's age discrimination. What is it going to take to stop this? Do I have to sue?"

"Don't let your pride endanger yourself or one of your teammates," she said. "Instead of trying to keep up with people thirty years younger, use that experience of yours to coordinate our rescue efforts, analyze situations and communicate with other agencies. We could really use someone like that, and you would be perfect for the job." She had no idea where the idea had come from, but she saw it was the perfect solution. Normally, people rotated through the role of incident commander, but Ted would be ideal for the position, as long as he didn't let a fantasy that he was still an athlete in his prime get in the way.

"Don't patronize me," he said.

"I'm not patronizing," she said. She would have to talk to Tony about this, and the others, too, but it could be a great innovation that would benefit everyone. "At least consider it," she said. "What would a role as full-time incident commander look like to you?"

He was shaking his head when both their phones went off. She pulled out hers and read the text: Missing hiker, Grizzly Ridge.

"Looks like we got a missing hiker," Ted said.

"I'm calling for details now." As she waited for dispatch to answer, she shoved her feet into boots and found her keys. "I'll meet you at headquarters, Ted," she said. "We'll talk about this later."

Her mother came into the living room, Carrie's SAR parka and pack in her hands. "I heard your phone," Becky said. She glanced at Ted. "Hello, Ted. Are you going to ride with Carrie?"

"I have my own car." He opened the door. "See you there."

"Thanks, Mom." Carrie took the jacket and pack as the dispatcher, Rayanne, said, "Hey Carrie. You've got a fifty-four-year-old male and a fifty-two-year-old female, married couple from Dallas, George and Angela Dempsey, who set out to hike Grizzly Ridge this afternoon. They were supposed to meet friends for dinner and never showed and their vehicle is still at the trailhead."

"Any medical conditions we should know about?" Carrie asked as she slipped on the parka.

"Kids say not. They're both healthy, though there's always the altitude to consider."

"Right. Thanks. We'll get right on it." She ended the call, her mind racing with a running list of procedures and equipment they might need. It would be dark soon and that meant the temperature was dropping fast. If one or both of the couple were injured, the team would have to bring them down a rugged trail along an exposed ridge in the dark. If they were lost, they might have to suspend the search until daylight in order to protect the searchers. Going off-piste in winter darkness without knowing exactly where they should head would be foolish.

And that, Carrie realized as she started her car, was what she should have told her mother. She wasn't being a coward about relationships. Instead, she was being prudent. She wasn't acting only for herself anymore. She had Amber and Dylan to protect as well. By limiting her risks, she was really looking out for them all.

Chapter Five

"We need a hasty team to head up the Grizzly Ridge Trail ahead of the main group," Carrie addressed the team at search and rescue headquarters as they gathered gear for the search for missing hikers George and Angela Dempsey. "Danny, I want you with me, and we need one other person."

"I'll go," Ted said.

"I want you to stay at the trailhead as incident commander," Carrie said.

"Sheri or Ryan can do that," Ted said. "I'll go with you."

Everyone else held their breath, Danny included. How was Carrie going to handle what bordered on insubordination? Tony would have shut Ted down or even sent him home. The struggle showed clearly on Carrie's face—give in to Ted and risk weakening her authority or get into an argument that could waste precious time?

"I'll be incident commander," Sheri said. "I don't mind."

"Fine," Carrie said. "Ted, you're with us. Get a move on, everyone."

Danny slid into the passenger seat in Carrie's SUV, while Ted climbed into the rear. He could have cut the tension with a scalpel, but he didn't know how to diffuse the situation. Ted had been out of line, but making a big deal out of it probably would have made things worse.

Ted acted as if nothing had happened. He sat forward as Carrie sped out of the parking area and said, "There's a place two-thirds of the way up Grizzly Ridge trail where there's a lot of beetle-kill pine. If one of those trees came down, it would block it and force a detour. It's a likely place for someone who isn't familiar with the trail to get offtrack."

"I'll keep that in mind," Carrie said. She signaled the turn onto the county road that led to the trailhead and switched on the wipers. A mix of rain and ice had begun to spit from the sky. "This moisture is liable to be snow farther up on that trail," she said.

"Hypothermia risk, for sure," Danny said, mentally running through his supply of instant hot packs and blankets in his medical kit.

"There's a ledge about two miles up that trail with a northern exposure," Ted said. "If we don't find these folks before then, we should check around there in case one of them slipped and fell."

"Thanks, Ted," Carrie said. "We'll do that."

"This is why you need me with you instead of back at the trailhead," he said. "No one else on the team has my knowledge of these trails."

"Knowledge you could have passed on as incident

commander," Carrie said. Her hands tightened on the steering wheel, knuckles whitening.

"Showing is better than talking," he said. "You'll see."

They made the rest of the drive in silence. Carrie parked at the trailhead next to a white Toyota 4Runner with a camper shell—the Dempseys' vehicle. As the three of them climbed out of the car, a Rayford County sheriff's black-and-white SUV pulled in and Sgt. Gage Walker got out. "Anything you need from me?" he asked.

"Not yet, anyway," Carrie said as she shouldered a pack. She keyed her radio and hailed Sheri. "We're starting up now," Carrie said.

"Ten-four. I've got Ryan, Jake, and Eldon headed your way."

"Tell them to stage at the trailhead until we know what we'll need and where," Carrie said.

She hooked the radio to the shoulder strap of her pack and started up the trail. The precipitation was steadier now, thin pellets of ice that stung Danny's bare cheeks and danced hypnotically in the beam of his headlamp. The frozen mud was slick underfoot with a fresh crust of ice. They traveled at a slow jog, and it wasn't long before he heard Ted's labored breathing as the older man brought up the rear of their trio.

Carrie stopped abruptly and looked back. "Ted, are you all right?" she asked.

"I'm fine," he gasped. "I'll get my second wind in a minute. Keep going."

Carrie started out again, feet pounding the trail. Danny made a mental note not to challenge her to a race anytime soon. He did trail running to keep in shape, but he was having a hard time matching her pace.

After a hundred yards of switchbacks the trail leveled out, still climbing, but at a less punishing rate. Carrie stopped and unstrapped a hailer from her pack. "George!" she shouted. "Angela!"

They waited, but only silence—and Ted's still ragged breathing—greeted them.

Carrie repeated the calls twice more, waiting a full minute each time, but there was no answer. "We'll try again in a bit," she said, and set out jogging once more.

When she stopped again, Danny realized Ted was no longer behind him. "Where's Ted?" he asked. "Ted!" he shouted.

"I'm…coming." The reply came from some distance back. Danny glanced at Carrie, who stared down the trail, expression impassive.

It was a full two minutes before Ted staggered into view. He stopped and bent over, hands on his knees, gasping. Carrie checked her phone. "We've only come a mile," she said. "We have probably several more to go."

Ted looked up. His headlamp made seeing his expression impossible, but Danny heard the anger in his voice. "You're doing this on purpose," he said. "Trying to prove I'm no longer fit."

"I'm doing what a hasty team is supposed to do,"

Carrie said. "Our job is to get to the person in need of help as quickly as possible. It's why we do trail running as part of our training."

Ted said nothing.

Carrie took out the hailer again and called for George and Angela, again with no reply.

"We don't even know where these people are or what's wrong with them," Ted said. "There's no need to run."

"We don't know," Carrie said. "But we know the odds are they are either injured or lost, or both. It's how the majority of these calls play out, so we respond accordingly. Let's go."

She turned and headed out again, slowing a little as they reached a steeper section, through stands of dead trees, the black trunks glittering with ice in the glow of their headlamps.

"Is this where you thought they might have become lost?" Carrie asked.

But once more Ted had fallen behind and didn't answer. Neither did the Dempseys.

"There aren't any trees down on the trail," Carrie said. She took out a flashlight and played its beam along the route. "Do you see any boot prints that look fresh enough to have been made today? I wish I knew for sure they came this way."

Danny joined her in the search. They spotted a couple of clear prints rimmed with ice—one large enough to be a man's and a smaller one with shallower treads that probably belonged to a woman. "That could be them," Danny said. They stood very close, staring down at the prints. He smelled peppermint on her breath—gum or toothpaste or maybe lip balm? "Should I go back to look for Ted?" he asked.

"I guess so," she said. "I hope he hasn't had a heart attack."

But a wavering beam of light, accompanied by muttered swearing, announced Ted's arrival. He leaned against a tree trunk and drew out a water bottle but failed in an attempt to unscrew the cap and just stood there, eyes closed, body sagging.

Alarmed, Danny raced to him. "Sit down," he instructed, and helped his friend slide down the tree trunk until he was in a sitting position on the wet ground. He checked the older man's pulse—strong but irregular. Ted's skin was clammy. "Are you having any chest pain?" Danny asked.

"I'm not having a heart attack," Ted said.

Carrie ignored him. "Danny, will Ted be all right waiting here by himself for a bit?" she asked.

"Let me check him out." He examined Ted, despite the older man's weak attempts to push him away and grumbles that he was fine. When he was satisfied, Danny stepped back. "He's taxed, but he's not having a heart attack. But I don't think it's a good idea in these conditions to have anyone hiking by themselves."

Carrie nodded and turned back to Ted. "I need you to wait here," she said. "I'm going to radio for someone to come up and go back down with you. I don't think it's safe for you to go on, and I don't want you heading down on your own. Not in your condition."

Ted's protest consisted mostly of swearing. Carrie didn't even blink. "I don't have time to argue. I'm ordering you to stay here." She keyed her radio and made her request for someone to fetch Ted.

"I'll send Eldon," Sheri said.

"Thanks," Carrie said. She turned to Danny. "Are you ready to go on?"

He nodded. It was probably a testament to how beaten Ted was that he didn't say anything as they moved on without him.

Neither of them said anything until the top of the next set of switchbacks, where the trail finally leveled off to traverse the top of the ridge Ted had mentioned before. "You're sure Ted will be okay by himself?" she asked. "I'm furious with him right now, but I definitely don't want him to die."

"No guarantees," Danny said. "But I think he's in good condition for a man his age, with no history of heart trouble. And Eldon will get to him in less than an hour, probably."

"I should have insisted he stay at the trailhead," she said. "Tony would have."

"Ted might not have opposed Tony so openly," Danny said.

"You think he was trying me out because I'm a woman?" she asked. "Or because this is my first time as captain?"

"Both, probably."

"He came by my house this evening," she said.

That surprised Danny. "What did he want?"

"He wanted to complain about being discriminated against because of his age. He said Tony was trying to push him out. He was upset that Sheri was chosen as training officer instead of him."

"What did you tell him?"

"I tried to emphasize how important his experience and knowledge of the area and of search and rescue history in Eagle Mountain are to the group. And I tried to persuade him that the best way to utilize that experience and knowledge was as incident commander."

"That makes a lot of sense," Danny said.

"He hated the idea. And you saw how he reacted when I suggested he take that role tonight. He put himself in danger and he's left us short one person."

"I'm glad I'm not you right now," he said. "But for what it's worth, I think you're doing a good job. With Ted and with everything else that has happened—the vandalism and stuff. You're exactly the person we need right now." It had been a revelation, seeing this aspect of her personality emerge. Before, she had been the attractive woman who had turned him down. Now he had a much more complex view of her.

"Thanks. That means a lot." She let out a deep breath. "And now we really need to find the Dempseys. It's miserable out here." She raised the hailer once more. "Angela Dempsey! George Dempsey!"

No answer. Carrie tried again. "Angela! Geor—"

"Help! Please help!" The woman's voice was high-pitched and tinged with panic.

"Angela! Is that you?" Carrie called.

"Yes! George fell and is hurt and I couldn't leave him."

"Where are you?" Carrie asked.

"On a ledge below the trail. He slipped on the ice. I climbed down, but I can't get back up."

"Keep talking to me. We're with Eagle Mountain Search and Rescue and we're coming to help." She lowered the inhaler and looked at Danny, smiling. "We found them," she said softly.

"Almost." He pulled a large Maglite with a spotlight beam from his pack and switched it on, then aimed it to their left, on the downhill side of the trail. He and Carrie walked slowly forward, staring at each area lit by the beam, until it came to rest on the white face of a woman thirty feet below. She stood and waved both hands at them. A darker shape lay on the ground beside her. "Thank God you're here," Angela Dempsey said.

"Stay right there," Carrie said. "We'll come to you. This is Danny. He's a nurse. He's going to ask you about your husband's injuries."

"I think his leg is broken," Angela said.

"Which leg?" Danny asked.

"Um…left."

"Can you see bone protruding from the skin?"

"No. He just…landed funny. And he said he heard something pop. And he's in a lot of pain."

"I'm in pain. I'm not dead." The man's voice—George's—was strong. "And I'm freezing my tuchus off out here."

Danny grinned. "We'll see if we can get you warmed up. Hang on a little bit."

Carrie was already on the radio with Sheri, relating the Dempseys' situation. They'd need climbing gear to get the couple off the ledge, materials to stabilize George's leg and a litter to transport him down the mountain. Hot food and coffee for all of them. An ambulance waiting to transport.

Danny and Carrie spent the next hour talking with the Dempseys, trying to keep their spirits up. They were able to lower blankets and hot packs to them and promised more help was on the way.

Jake was the first to arrive. He jogged up the trail, bringing an air cast for George's fractured leg and some of the gear they would need to safely move him back onto the trail.

"I came up with Eldon," he said as he slipped his pack from his back. "He's taking Ted back down. What happened? Ted looks terrible and he was cussing a blue streak."

"Never mind Ted," Carrie said. "We've got to set up to get Danny down to the Dempseys on that ledge."

"Are you going to go with him?" Jake asked.

The idea of climbing down there in the icy dark made her heart beat a little too fast. Of course she would do it if she had to, but in this case, she didn't have to. "No, I'm going to wait for the others."

"They're on their way." He began unloading the rest of the gear and laying out the ropes and other climbing gear. He worked quickly and competently, impressive for someone who had been training only a few weeks.

Approaching voices announced the arrival of Ryan, and Hannah. They set to work, everyone knowing their roles in getting this couple back to safety. Danny and Hannah climbed down to George and Angela, where they were able to stabilize George's fracture and give him some pain relief. Thermoses of hot coffee and soup warmed them, then they assisted Angela in the climb up to the trail and brought up George's litter. Then everyone fell into line for the trek back down the mountain. Carrie brought up the rear, doing a last check that they had left no equipment or debris behind.

It was after 2:00 a.m. by the time they saw George, accompanied by Angela, loaded into the waiting ambulance. "That went about as smoothly as a rescue could," Sheri said as they watched the taillights of the ambulance dissolve into the darkness.

"It did," Carrie agreed. The adrenaline of the rescue effort had faded, leaving her bone-tired and craving warmth and sleep.

"What happened with Ted?" Sheri asked. "He just glared at me when I asked, and insisted Eldon drive him back to headquarters right then."

"He couldn't keep up on the trail," Carrie said. "I should have made him stay down here in the first place, but I didn't want to waste time arguing with him. As it is, he could have been seriously hurt, and the rescue would have been delayed even further. I should have stood up to him and I didn't."

"Ted is stubborn enough he might have tried to follow us anyway." Danny joined them. He looked as weary as Carrie felt, shadows under his eyes, skin abnormally pale in the glare of the work lights set up at the trailhead. "At least having him with us allowed me to monitor him. He's in better shape than most men his age, but he wasn't up to running that trail."

"If he can't do the job, he shouldn't be on the team," Sheri said. "If he can't be depended on to pull his weight, he puts other people in danger."

"He has a lot of experience and knowledge," Carrie said. "I thought that could be put to good use as incident commander."

"But everyone has to be prepared to step in and take an active role," Sheri said. "If Ted can't do that, it's time to retire."

Carrie nodded. "I know. And Ted probably knows it, too. I'll talk to Tony about it when I see him tomorrow."

Sheri nodded and moved to help Ryan take down the lights. Carrie started to join them, but Danny put a hand on her shoulder. "You're doing a good job," he said. "Don't second-guess yourself."

She told herself it was only because she was so tired that tears stung her eyes at his words. "Thanks," she managed, and quickly turned away. She felt too vulnerable to face him right now. Too close to revealing how much she needed those words. How much she wanted someone to care. That that someone would be

Danny—the serial dater, who went through women the way some people adopted and abandoned hobbies… It was too depressing to think about.

Chapter Six

When Danny had suggested he accompany Carrie to visit Tony in the hospital on Monday, he halfway expected her to tell him she was tired of him tagging along. It wasn't as if the two of them had been close before Tony's accident. They had been thrown together a lot since then and he was surprised how well they got along.

"What do you like to do for fun?" he asked as they set out for Junction Monday afternoon. He had a half day of comp time he needed to use up before the quarter ended and had decided today would be a good day to clock out early. Carrie was driving them again. She seemed to like being behind the wheel and he was happy to let her. Her SUV was more comfortable than his old Honda anyway.

"Fun?" She glanced at him, one eyebrow raised in question.

"Do you have hobbies?" he asked. "Things you like to do to relax?"

She laughed, though the sound wasn't exactly joyful. "You have obviously never been a parent. I don't have time for hobbies. Or relaxing."

"That doesn't sound very healthy," he said, then wanted to take back the words. "I mean, I don't see how you do it all."

"Yeah, well, I don't do it all. Not well." She smoothed her palms down the steering wheel. "I guess search and rescue is my stress relief. Not that it isn't intense sometimes, but it gets me out of my own head. And it feels really good to help other people, you know?"

"I know," he said. "When I signed up I thought I would just do it for a while, to help out in a pinch, but I got hooked. And hey, it impresses women."

"Yeah, I'm so impressed."

He laughed, and she did, too, a real laugh this time. He found himself searching for a way to make her laugh again. "Yeah, they're always impressed when they find out I save lives in my spare time. And then I have to cancel a date because I get a callout and they aren't so amused. After the second or third time that happens, they're moving on."

"One more reason not to bother dating," she said.

Was she saying she never dated? That he wasn't the only man she had turned down? Because surely others had asked her out. "I like being single," he said. "But I'd rather not be alone all the time. So I guess the pluses and minuses even out."

"I'm not alone," she said. "I live with my mom and two children. There are days when I'd pay for a few hours to myself."

Did he detect a bit of false bravado behind her words? "I could give up dating," he said. "But I'd really miss sex."

A pink blush lit her cheeks. “Um, well, yeah, there is that.”

He wondered how long it had been since a man had held her intimately. She had a combination of femininity and strength a lot of men would be drawn to. A sensuality beneath her no-nonsense veneer. Then he told himself he shouldn’t be thinking about her this way.

He looked away, at the first spring wildflowers beginning to splash the roadside with pinks and purples, blooming despite patches of snow. Probably time to change the subject. “I don’t guess you’ve heard anything else from the sheriff’s department about the fire that destroyed the Beast.”

“Nothing,” she said. “And nothing on Austen’s accident, though maybe Jake is right and it was just a driver being a little reckless on a snowy day.”

“I don’t think what happened with Tony was an accident,” Danny said. “It’s going to make me even more nervous about climbing.”

“Me too. We’ll just have to be extra cautious when it comes to inspecting our gear.” She slowed as they reached the edge of Junction. “I wish I had something to tell Tony,” she said. “When I talked to him on the phone yesterday, he said he doesn’t remember the moments leading up to his fall, but he’s sure he would have said something if he noticed anyone tampering with SAR gear.”

“Maybe he’ll remember something today,” Danny said.

A short drive around the south side of town took

them to the hospital. This time they bypassed the information desk and went straight to the elevator and rode the car up to the patient floor where Tony had been transferred.

They found him sitting in a wheelchair by his bed, still hampered by casts and looking pale and almost frail, in a green hospital gown, wire-rimmed glasses magnifying his blue eyes. His beard was neatly trimmed, damp hair curling around his ears. “It’s great to see you out of bed,” Carrie said, and leaned down to give him an awkward hug. “You look better already.”

“I’m a mess, but it’s better than being dead,” Tony said. He nodded to Danny. “Have they found out who did this to me yet?”

“We haven’t heard anything,” Carrie said.

“Can you think of anyone who was upset enough with you in particular or with SAR in general to have damaged those ropes?” Danny asked. He leaned against the end of the hospital bed, facing Tony.

“I’ve had plenty of time to think about it and I can’t come up with even one person.” Tony frowned at the cast on his right leg, propped in front of him, rigid and off-white and uncomfortable looking. “Maybe it was just someone random.”

“Someone who had access to our equipment,” Danny reminded him. None of them wanted to think that someone close to the organization would do something like this, but ignoring the possibility didn’t make it any less so.

"Ted has been upset about how some issues are being handled with search and rescue," Carrie said.

"What makes you say that?" Tony asked.

"He came to see me at home yesterday evening," she said. "He complained about being passed over for the training officer position and said you were trying to push him out altogether."

Tony scowled. "I'm not trying to push him out. But it's clear he's not up to some of the physical challenges we face. I wanted to work with him to find a role that would focus on his skills without hampering the rest of us."

"Ted's always been a bit of a curmudgeon," Danny said. "But do you really think he would do something like this?"

Tony's face slackened with shock. "I can't believe Ted would hurt someone," he said. "He's devoted to Eagle Mountain SAR. He helped found the group." He studied Carrie's face. "Do you seriously think Ted put acid on my ropes and burned the Beast?"

She shifted from foot to foot. "I don't know. But he was pretty angry yesterday. He accused us of age discrimination and threatened to sue."

Tony's eyes widened. "He's a lot more upset than I thought. Were you able to calm him down?"

"Not really. I suggested that with his experience, he'd be really valuable as our incident commander, but that only made him angrier. We got a call last night to search for a couple of missing hikers and Ted insisted on being part of the hasty team."

"How did he do?" Tony asked.

"It was awful. Danny and I jogged up the Grizzly Ridge Trail and Ted couldn't keep up. I was afraid he was going to have a heart attack and ended up ordering him to wait for someone to come up and take him back down to the trailhead. That meant we were two people short. I never should have let him try to come with us. I know you wouldn't have."

"Maybe letting him realize the limits of his capabilities that way was a good thing," Tony said. "Have you talked to him today?"

"I tried to call him this morning to see how he was doing but he didn't answer," she said. "I left a message, but he hasn't responded. I wondered if he was upset enough to want to lash out at us all."

"He was late to the meeting Sunday morning," Danny said. "He showed up only a little while before Austen did." He turned to Tony. "Austen was delayed because another car ran his off the road."

"Ted said he was late because of the weather," Carrie said. "It was snowing pretty hard."

"He could have waited until he saw Austen's vehicle approaching and raced down the hill to run him into the ditch, then turned around and drove to the meeting as if nothing happened," Danny said. The idea that Ted, someone he had always liked and even looked up to, would do something like that made him physically ill.

"We shouldn't jump to conclusions," Tony said. "Ted is a lot of things, but I've never known him to be violent. And he really is devoted to SAR. I can't see him wanting to destroy it."

"I'm sure you're right," she said. "Now I feel bad even bringing it up. I just wish we knew who was responsible. With your fall and losing the Beast to arson and the attack on Austen, I'm holding my breath, afraid of what will happen next."

"We're all on edge," Danny said. "But that will make it harder for whoever this is to do anything else."

"What are you doing about a new search and rescue vehicle?" Tony asked.

"The insurance company is sending us a check for $5,000," she said. "It's not nearly enough, but more than I expected, honestly. And Sheri is working with some others to come up with ideas for raising money."

"We should ask the county to chip in," Tony said. "They're always saying they don't have any money, but they should contribute to this. Everyone in the county, not to mention a lot of visitors, benefit from the work we do."

"Maybe when you're home again, you can speak to county officials," Carrie said.

"Why wait?" Tony said. "I don't have anything else to do between rehab sessions. I'll start making calls now."

Carrie brightened. "That would be terrific."

Tony looked up, over her shoulder. "Speaking of rehab." He raised his voice. "Here comes my favorite torturer now."

A petite redhead in blue scrubs glided into the room. "Time to get back to work, Mr. Meisner," she said.

"Mr. Meisner is my old man," Tony said.

"All right, Tony." She grinned. "Say goodbye to your friends and quit goofing off."

"No rest for the weary." Tony shook his head. "Thanks for stopping by, and keep me posted on developments."

"We will," Carrie said.

She and Danny left the room. He waited until they were in her car again before he spoke. "Do you really think Ted could be behind these attacks?" he asked.

She started the SUV and backed out of her parking slot. "All I know is that he was truly angry when he came to my house yesterday. And you saw him last night—he was furious."

Danny nodded. He had dismissed Ted's rage last night as typical of the older man, who had a reputation for salty language and a short fuse. But would he really go so far as to hurt Tony—his friend and someone he had known since Tony was a teenager? "I guess all we can do is keep an eye on him," he said. "Make note of anything suspicious." He glanced at her. Tendrils of hair had come loose from her braid and curled around her cheeks. His fingers itched to brush them back so he could see her expression more clearly. And to feel if her skin was as soft as it looked. "Just to be safe, maybe you shouldn't be alone with Ted for the time being," he said, his voice coming out rougher than he intended.

She glanced at him. "Oh, I don't think Ted would hurt me."

"If he hurt Tony because he was upset with Tony's assignments, why wouldn't he go after you after last night?" The idea chilled him. "You said yourself he was furious. And he blamed you for putting him on the spot."

She huffed out a breath. "You have a point but don't worry. Like I said before, it's rare that I'm ever alone. I work in an office full of people, my mom and kids are around when I'm home, and on a search and rescue call, I have the whole team around me. So I guess I'm safe."

"You're alone with me now."

Silence. She braked for a red light, then turned to look at him. "I am, aren't I?" Her lips curved in a slow smile. "But you don't scare me, Danny."

"That's good." He settled back into his seat. He'd never tell her, but when he was being honest, she scared him just a little, the way she unsettled him, and made him think about her the way he had never thought about another woman. As if the idea of her being hurt, by Ted or anyone else, caused a physical pain. He wasn't that kind of man, but it seemed with her, he was.

CARRIE WAS IN the middle of a meeting at work Tuesday morning when her silenced phone buzzed against her hip. She ignored it and tried to focus on what the senior partner, Greg Abernathy, was saying about changes the client wanted to a proposed condo development north of Eagle Mountain. "If we put the community room where he wants it, that will eat up half a dozen parking spaces, at least," Carrie said. "He'll be out of compliance with the county regulations for a new development."

"The client thinks he can get a variance," Greg said. "Our job is to draw up the plans the way he wants them so he can take them to the county."

Right, and the implied message was that Carrie, as the junior architect, was to keep her mouth shut and do as she was told. Which she would, because this was the only architectural firm in town and she had negotiated a flexible schedule that allowed her to take off early or work from home when her children needed her or she had a callout from search and rescue. Greg had told her when he hired her that he liked the idea of having a young woman on staff because it made the company looked progressive—as if she was a generic placeholder labeled Token Female instead of a talented architect in her own right.

But being close to home and available was more important than acknowledgment of her skill, she reminded herself as the meeting ended and she headed back to her office.

Another perk of the job was that she had an office to herself—what had probably once been a bedroom in the old Victorian home on Main Street. The room had good light, polished hardwood floors and plenty of room for a desk and a drafting table. And a door that shut so she could have privacy when needed.

She slipped her phone from her pocket and frowned at the number. Local but unfamiliar. She hit the button to call back and was startled when a brisk female voice answered. "Rayford County Sheriff's Department."

"Oh, um, hello. This is Carrie Andrews. I missed a call from this number."

"One moment."

Instrumental music of a song she didn't recognize replaced the woman's voice, then a man said. "Hello, Carrie. Thanks for calling me."

She recognized this voice—Deputy Jake Gwynn, "Has something else happened related to search and rescue?" she asked.

"We've received the reports back on the fire that destroyed the Jeep and the tests done on the climbing rope," Jake said. "When can you stop by and talk to us about it?"

She glanced at the clock. She was supposed to get off at four today to attend Dylan's youth lacrosse game. If she left at three thirty she should be able to talk to Jake and get to the game on time or close to it. "Can you meet me at three thirty?" she asked.

"That's fine. You're welcome to bring someone else from search and rescue with you, if you like."

They said goodbye and she stared at the phone in her hand. She thought about calling Danny and asking if he wanted to meet her at the sheriff's department, but she immediately rejected the idea. He was probably working, and besides, she didn't need Danny to hold her hand through all of this, though it felt like that was exactly what he had been doing so far. Maybe not holding her hand, but certainly supporting her, providing a sounding board for her concerns and offering encouragement when she needed it.

Not a role she would ever have pictured for Danny

Irwin. Sure, he was a competent caregiver and member of the search and rescue team, but he was also a flirt who fit the mold of so many other men in this town—ski bums, rock hounds and bike jocks who lived to play and prided themselves on avoiding commitment but also stress. They were good-looking, charming and fit, and thus always had a woman for company when they needed one, but none of those relationships lasted long. Wives and kids would only cramp their style.

Come to think of it, Hannah had dated Danny for a while, before she met Jake. They had managed to break things off with little awkwardness, probably because Danny had never let things get serious.

A good example for Carrie to follow. Not that she would ever get serious about Danny. She wasn't that foolish. From one perspective, he might have been a perfect match for her. He was handsome, easygoing and about her age. They shared a common interest in search and rescue. And best of all, like her, he wasn't interested in a long-term commitment. It might be nice to have someone to go out with, someone with whom she could share dinner or movies. And sex. She grew warmer, remembering how he had brought up the subject yesterday. Women talked, and they especially talked about men, and she had heard that Danny was, well, talented in bed.

But she knew herself too well. She couldn't give the rest of herself without handing over her heart, too. She didn't think she was capable of the kind of no-strings-attached relationship men like Danny specialized in. Spending so much time with him lately had been nice, and she was developing a certain fondness for the man. She just had to remember not to let that go too far.

At the sheriff's department that afternoon, Carrie waited less than a minute before Jake came out to meet her. A slender man with short, dark brown hair and brown eyes that were almost black, he was training to work with search and rescue, but he hadn't yet participated in many calls, so Carrie didn't know him well. "Thanks for stopping by," he said. "Come right through here."

She followed him through the door and down the hall, trying not to stare at everything they passed. This was the first time she had ever been in a law enforcement office and she felt a little nervous.

Jake stopped at a door and knocked, and a familiar voice said, "Come in."

Sheriff Travis Walker stood from behind his desk. "Hello, Carrie," he said.

"Hello." Nerves made the word come out a little shaky. No reason for her to be nervous, she reminded herself, but why was the sheriff involved in what she had assumed would be a simple report?

"Sit down." Jake gestured to a chair in front of the sheriff's desk and he moved a second chair over beside her while Travis resumed his seat.

The sheriff's desk was neater than her own, with only a laptop, a tiered In and Out box and a framed photo of Travis's wife, Lacy, a beautiful brunette standing in a mountain meadow.

Jake opened a folder on the desk in front of him. "The arson investigator concluded the search and rescue Jeep was deliberately set on fire," he said. "Unfortunately, the fire destroyed any forensic evidence the arsonist might have left, and we haven't found witnesses who saw anyone near the Jeep before the fire."

"SAR headquarters is pretty remote," Travis said. "The arsonist could be fairly confident no one would see him or her."

"Does SAR remember seeing anyone around that evening who shouldn't have been there?" Jake asked.

"No. Everyone had left headquarters hours before. I was in Junction, at the hospital with Tony Meisner. Another volunteer, Danny Irwin, was with me."

"So someone might have gone back to headquarters after everyone left and no one would have seen them?" Travis asked.

"I guess so." She had to force herself to admit this was true. "There aren't any other buildings around headquarters, and no one lives up that road, so it doesn't get much traffic."

Jake flipped to another page in the folder. "We also received the results for the lab analysis of the climbing rope Tony was using. The fibers were soaked in hydrochloric acid, also known as muriatic acid."

"I've heard of it," she said. "But I don't know much about it."

"I spoke with some experienced climbers, and with the lab," Jake said. "For someone not to notice the damage upon your initial inspection, and for Tony to have gotten as far into the canyon as he did, we believe the acid must have been poured onto the ropes either immediately before or immediately after he inspected them. But probably immediately before."

"But we were all there," she said. "Somebody would have seen any tampering with the ropes."

"Not necessarily," Jake said. "We're talking maybe half a cup of acid. A person could carry that in a small vial or bottle in their pocket and tip it onto the rope without anyone noticing. Was there a particular team member helping Tony that day?"

She tried to remember. "We were all assisting each other," she said. "I was getting into my climbing gear, waiting my turn to descend. Danny and Tony were going to go down together, spaced along the canyon rim. Sheri, as training officer, was supervising all of us. Ryan and Austen and Eldon and Ted were helping everyone else. And Hannah was there, too." She shrugged. "You should talk to Tony. He told me he doesn't remember anything about that day, but maybe his memories will start to return."

"I will talk to him," Jake said. "Was there anyone else in the area that day—somebody not part of the SAR training exercise?"

"No."

"You're sure?" Travis asked.

"I'm sure. We always clear the area of other people before we start, but that morning there wasn't anyone else to clear. We had the canyon to ourselves." She swallowed hard as the meaning behind that admission sank in. "So whoever poured that acid on the ropes, it had to be one of us."

"Do you have reason to believe somebody wanted to harm Tony?" Jake asked. "Maybe a volunteer he had argued with?"

"No. Nothing like that." Even as she said it an image of Ted, accusing Tony of trying to push him out, popped into her head. But she couldn't believe Ted would do something like this. It was too...calculating. "Where would someone get muriatic acid?" she asked.

"You can buy it at most hardware stores," Travis said. "They use it to etch concrete."

She shuddered at the idea of something like that eating through rope fibers.

"We'll ask at the local stores," Jake said. "But it's the kind of item someone might already have at home."

This whole conversation felt surreal. She shook her head, as if that could somehow settle her thoughts into a semblance of order. "What about Austen's accident?" she asked. "Did you find anything there?"

"No," Jake said. "It was snowing too hard to draw conclusions. And we don't really have evidence to link that with the Jeep or the damaged ropes. It's a steep road and it was snowing hard when he ran into the ditch. It's possible someone made a wrong turn, and in heading back down the mountain, they were going too fast for the weather and panicked when Austen drove toward them. There was no damage to his vehicle. He simply slid into the ditch, bumped his head and dented a fender." He closed the folder. "That's all we have now. Let us know if you think of anything that might help us in our investigation."

"Of course." She stood, anxious to be out of here.

Jake escorted her back to the lobby, where she muttered goodbye and fled. As she drove toward the ball fields, his words replayed in her head. What kind of information, exactly, would be useful? The search and rescue team was like a family—siblings and cousins who mostly got along but sometimes disagreed, said things they shouldn't say or displayed fits of temper. That only proved they were human, not people who would destroy a valuable vehicle or try to kill their captain.

Except one of them was. Icy fear gripped her at the thought, and she held more tightly to the steering wheel to control the shaking that overtook her. Someone had tried to kill Tony. Would he—or she—try to finish the job, or target someone else? Were they all in danger from one of their own?

Chapter Seven

After seven years at the surgical center, Danny had the routines of his job burned into his body. Every procedure had a protocol to follow, and he had a knack for placating even the most difficult patients. He liked the work, but mostly he liked what else the job enabled him to do. Working three twelve-hour shifts a week allowed him plenty of time off and a salary large enough to support his interests. Over the years he had seen various coworkers come and go, many to take better positions at hospitals or other facilities. Danny didn't mind that there wasn't a lot of room for advancement where he was. He found his challenges in other areas of his life, not at his job.

Wednesday evening as he prepared to drive home after work, he checked the weather forecast on his phone, a habit he had developed since joining search and rescue. Rescue calls had seasonal patterns: summer saw more lost hikers, accidents on Jeep roads in the high country and swift-water rescues on local rivers. Deepest winter brought more ice-climbing accidents, missing backcountry skiers and traffic mishaps on icy roads.

Now, in late March, was an in-between time, with periods of heavy, wet snow broken by stretches of warmer, sunny days. This was avalanche season, and a time when hikers and mountain climbers, eager to hit the trails after a long winter, sometimes got caught by the ice and snow that still lay deep at higher elevations. A few more weeks and they could add in mudslides and rock slides and rivers flooded by snowmelt to the list of potential hazards.

Tonight's forecast called for temperatures just above freezing. Snowmelt that had run onto the roads would refreeze into black ice. SAR would be lucky to make it through the week without at least one callout.

An hour later, he was just pulling the plastic film from a microwave lasagna when his phone's message alert sounded. He set aside his dinner and read the brief summary—a car had slid off the highway near the top of Dixon Pass. Danny stuck the lasagna back into the refrigerator and went to round up his gear. A few minutes earlier, he had been thinking about how tired he was after being on his feet all day, but now the familiar adrenaline buzz kicked in, fizzing in his body as he anticipated what they might find at the accident scene. The message hadn't said where the car went off, but there were a couple of likely locations, spots known to be particularly hazardous, especially for ice. Whoever had been in the vehicle would need medical care, provided they survived the trip into the canyon.

Fifteen minutes later, he joined the rest of the team at SAR headquarters. Or rather, the portion of the team who were available. "We're shorthanded tonight," Carrie informed them as they gathered around her to get the details of this call. "Tony is still in the hospital, of course, but Hannah is also sick with the flu. Sheri and her husband are in Denver. I've asked Jake to join us to help make up numbers."

Jake Gwynn lifted a hand in greeting.

"Where's Ted?" Austen asked, looking around at the group, which consisted of Carrie, Jake, Danny, Ryan, Eldon and Austen.

"Ted isn't responding to my calls," Carrie said. She picked up her pack. "Come on. We should be able to go in two vehicles, with only six of us."

The blue-and-white strobes of two sheriff's department SUVs and a state highway patrol cruiser lit up the red rock walls that edged the highway on the climb up through Grizzly Creek Canyon, like a garish light show. A sign indicated the highway was closed, but the deputy on duty waved the search and rescue team through. Danny climbed out of Eldon's pickup and the sudden grip of cold made him suck in his breath.

Sgt. Gage Walker joined them by their vehicles. "A passing motorist saw the fresh skid marks and called it in," he said, and pointed toward the tire tracks that cut through old snow on the side of the highway, ending at the edge of a sheer drop-off. "I shined a handheld spotlight around and I can see what I think is the top of a vehicle," he continued. "I shouted, but nobody answered."

"We'll get a couple of people down there to take a look," Carrie said.

All of them except Jake had climbed in this area before. Eldon and Austen began hauling out the gear while Danny and Jake inspected everything. Danny made a point of sniffing the equipment for any hint of acid, but found nothing.

Carrie and Ryan unloaded a couple of litters, extra helmets, splints and other medical gear they might need. "An ambulance is on its way," Gage told them. "And we've got a medical helicopter on standby to land at the soccer fields if we need transport."

Right. The canyon was too narrow at this point to risk maneuvering a helicopter, especially at night. The ambulance could have a patient to the soccer fields in five minutes.

As the most qualified medical person on scene, Danny would go down first, along with Eldon. Carrie would remain up top as incident commander, while Ryan, Austen and Jake would handle the ropes and transport of any other gear.

Danny carried a medical pack with basic supplies, while Eldon hauled the chains and anchors they might need to stabilize the vehicle, if it had come to rest in a precarious position. They also had headlamps and hand-held lights to illuminate the accident scene as much as possible.

"Take your time and be careful," Carrie said as Danny indicated he was ready to start down.

He nodded. He didn't like climbing in daylight, when we could see what he was doing. At night, with ice slicking the surface of the rock, it was a matter of double-checking every move. He remembered watching Tony and being envious of the way he swung out over obstacles and skimmed down sheer rock walls. Danny moved at a crab's pace in contrast. A very slow crab, but one who would arrive at his destination alive and unharmed.

The car, a minivan, lay on its side on a rock ledge halfway to the river below, the passenger door wedged hard against a slanting pine tree that grew from the ledge. Eldon and Danny stopped above the ledge and swept their spotlights over the scene. "Hello!" Eldon shouted, and the sound came back at them, hollow and distorted. "Hello! Can anyone in the van hear me?" he called again.

"Help! Somebody please help!"

"We're coming down to help you!" Danny shouted. "Hang on tight." He tucked away the light and started climbing down again, toward the van. He landed on the ledge just behind Eldon, Together, they chocked the van's tires, and Eldon slid under the vehicle to wrap a chain around an axle, then secured this around a boulder up against the canyon wall. That didn't guarantee the van would stay where it was, but it upped the odds.

As soon as Eldon nodded in his direction, Danny hoisted himself onto the front tire and leaned across the hood to shine a light through the windshield.

A man sat slumped forward, forehead against the steering wheel, the white mass of the deflated airbag surrounding him. Blood, like a trickle of chocolate syrup in the harsh light, matted the back of his head.

A cry of pain made Danny shift the light to the passenger seat, to the white face of a woman, a fall of dark hair obscuring one eye and cheek, her lips twisted in a grimace of pain. She lay against the door, the seat belt taut around her, forcing her head over at an odd angle. “Hang on, ma’am, I’m coming,” he said, and crawled back across the hood, toward the driver’s side door.

Eldon joined him and the two of them tugged at the door, which wouldn’t budge. It was probably locked, since most vehicles automatically locked once the car was in motion. Eldon pulled a metal bar from his pack, ordered the woman to close her eyes, then hit the driver’s-side window, shattering the glass. Danny brushed away the pebbled fragments, reached inside with a gloved hand and opened the door.

He stopped to assess the man first, aware of the woman sobbing just across from him. The man was breathing, and his pulse was strong, but he had obviously hit his head and was unconscious. He would need transport to the hospital. “Ma’am, I’m going to get the driver out where he’ll be more comfortable, then I’ll help you,” Danny said. “Can you tell me where you’re hurt?”

“My baby,” she wailed.

Danny looked around them. There was no sign of a car seat or anything having to do with a child in the car. “Where is the baby?” he asked, forcing his voice to remain calm even as panic climbed his throat. If the child had been thrown free, it could be anywhere. And if it was outside the vehicle and alive, it could be freezing to death.

"The baby!" the woman said again, and moaned and clutched at her stomach.

Danny directed the beam of his headlamp toward her, and his eyes widened as he took in the mound of her stomach. He swallowed and focused on remaining calm. "It's going to be okay," he said. "How far along are you in your pregnancy?"

"Thirty-seven weeks." She fixed her eyes on him—big brown eyes, shiny with tears. "It's not supposed to be here yet."

"Tell me what's going on." Danny looked at her over the man—her husband's?—inert body.

"I'm having this baby," she said, her voice sharp.

"You're having labor pains?" Danny asked.

"Yes!" She clutched herself again and moaned.

"Okay. Hang on. We're going to see to your husband, then take care of you and your baby. Just… hang on."

He and Eldon fixed a cervical collar and a backboard to the man, then got him out of the car and into a litter. They wrapped him in blankets and tucked in some chemical heat packs, then Danny radioed Carrie. "We've got a man, the driver, unconscious with a head wound. Send a couple people down with a litter to get him up and into the ambulance. The passenger is a woman. I'm getting ready to assess her, but she says she's thirty-seven weeks pregnant and in active labor."

"Well." A pause. "I assume you've delivered a baby before?"

"I work in a surgical center. Not labor and delivery."

"So you've never delivered a baby before?" Carrie asked.

"I have not." He had studied the subject in nursing school of course, and even seen a film detailing the process. But that was different from trying to bring a child into the world in the cold darkness in a frozen canyon. "Let me see how far her labor has progressed. With luck we have time to get her to the hospital, where she'll be more comfortable."

While Eldon attended to the man, Danny climbed back into the vehicle. His headlamp lit up the woman's terrified face. "Hi, I'm Danny," he said. "I'm a nurse with Eagle Mountain Search and Rescue. We're going to get you out of here, to somewhere safe." He studied her seat belt and decided the first order of business was to cut her out of it. "I'm going to cut this seat belt, then maybe we can get you free of the car."

He took out a tool designed for the purpose and sliced through the safety belt. The woman yelped as she fell back against the door, then the cry changed to a wail of pain.

Danny took her wrist and found her pulse. It was strong, but rapid. "What's your name?" he asked.

"Rosa," she said. "My husband! Is he—"

"He's going to be fine," Danny said. "He's got a bump on the head. Now, do you think you can climb out? I'll help you."

Rosa grabbed the dash and the side of her seat and

made an effort to haul herself up. Danny took hold of her upper arms and pulled, and together they managed to get her to the edge of the door, where she fell into Danny's arms, the hard curve of her abdomen pressed against him. He tried to steady her and keep her on her feet, but she sank to the ground. "Ohhhh!" she moaned.

Danny crouched beside her. "How far apart are your pains?" he asked.

Her eyes met his, wide and frightened. "Not far. This baby is going to come soon."

"Is this your first?" he asked.

She shook her head. "Third. The others were fast, too." She tipped back and lay on the ground, knees up. "I think I'm going to have this baby now."

Eldon moved over. "Should we get some blankets under her or something?"

"Yeah." Danny's hopes of getting her into a litter and out of the canyon before the child came were fading. "Let's do that, then I'll examine her."

They made a makeshift pallet while Rosa alternately moaned and cursed. Danny examined her and discovered she was well dilated, her water had broken and the baby's arrival did indeed seem imminent.

By this time Austen and Ryan had arrived and were arranging to send a litter with Rosa's husband along a line up to the canyon rim. Danny walked a few steps away and radioed Carrie. "Get the paramedics down here," he said. "This baby isn't going to wait."

"It could take a bit to get them harnessed up and

down to you," she said. "Can you handle it in the meantime?"

"I'll have to," he said. "She said this is her third child, so that should help." Maybe she'd even be able to tell him how best to assist her.

He returned to Rosa, who was moving restlessly. When he touched her shoulder, she let out a scream. "Do something!" she shouted.

His radio beeped with a new transmission. "The paramedics won't come down," Carrie said.

"What do you mean, they won't come down?"

"They said they're not trained as climbers and it's too risky. That's a valid point. How is the woman?"

"Um...uncomfortable." Rosa let out a new string of curses.

"All right. Then, I'm on my way."

"You?" he asked. "Have you delivered a baby before?"

"No, but I've had two of them, so I know a few things. Tell Eldon he needs to climb up and take over on this end while I help you."

"Okay. And thanks." He probably could have remembered enough of his training to deliver the baby successfully—after all, Rosa would do most of the work—but knowing Carrie would be here made him feel a whole lot better.

He focused on his patient again and managed to get Rosa to calm down enough to tell him more about her contractions and about her other two labors. Apparently, her first child had arrived after only five hours of labor and her second had been born in the van on the way to the hospital. "The kids are with my mom," she said between contractions. "My husband and I were supposed to be going on a date, and then we hit a patch of ice and went flying. I've never been so terrified in my life, then we landed so hard—I think it jolted the baby on its way out."

Danny examined her again and thought he could feel the baby's head. He looked up at Rosa, over the mound of her abdomen. "Are you warm enough?" he asked.

"Are you kidding?" she asked. "The cold is the last thing I'm thinking about."

Right. He was sweating himself, though more from nerves than heat.

Carrie touched down beside him on the ledge and he rushed to help her out of her harness. "Am I glad to see you," he said.

"Here." She thrust a bag into his hands. "The paramedics said we might need this."

He opened the bag and recognized a birthing kit. Search and rescue even had one—somewhere in the supply closet back at headquarters. "Great," he said, and began laying out the contents of the kit.

Carrie moved to Rosa's head and took her hand. "Hi, Rosa, I'm Carrie," she said. "Let's see if we can get this baby into the world to meet you."

Carrie murmured to Rosa through the next round of contractions, her voice soothing and positive. The words were meant for Rosa, but Danny felt their effect, too.

"I gotta push!" Rosa said.

"Then, you go ahead and push," Carrie said.

Danny checked on the baby's progress. "I can see the top of the head," he said, and moved into position to ease the child into the world.

Five minutes later his hands were full of a warm, wet, very-much-alive infant. The baby squirmed and let out a loud cry. Rosa began to sob, reaching for her son. Danny swaddled the tiny boy against the cold and placed him on Rosa's stomach, then wrapped them both in every blanket available. "We need to get them both somewhere warm, right away," he said.

Carrie nodded and stood to bark orders. Shortly thereafter, mother and baby were strapped securely into a litter and fastened to a long line, being hoisted out of the canyon.

Danny and Carrie remained below, gathering discarded wrappings and equipment and packing everything away. When that was done, he felt together enough to turn to her. "Thanks for coming down," he said. "I think having a woman with her really helped Rosa." He put his hands on her shoulders. "And it helped me, too. I was feeling way out of my comfort zone."

"You did great," she said. "I never would have known this was your first."

She had switched off her headlamp, and he tilted his up so that it didn't shine in her eyes but gave enough light to illuminate her face. Her cheeks were pink with cold, and her eyes shone with excitement. "What was it like when you had your two?" he asked, truly curious to know.

"Dylan was born on a rainy night in October and my husband and I were both terrified. I was at the hospital twenty hours before he made an appearance and by that time I was too exhausted to appreciate the moment. Amber was born at three in the afternoon after only six hours at the hospital and I had an epidural right away, so I got to kind of enjoy the process more." She shrugged. "I don't think most women remember too many details about the delivery. They're too focused on the little miracle they produced."

"Yeah." Even Danny, a single man, could appreciate how amazing birth was, though he hoped not to have to experience it quite so up close and personal again anytime soon. He put his arm around her and pulled her to him. She didn't tug away. It was just the two of them here in the darkness, and he had never felt closer to her, or to anyone, really. They stood there for a long moment, until she began to shiver with cold. "You ready to go up?" he asked.

"Yes." She radioed Jake to let him know they were on their way.

Weariness dragged at Danny as he pulled himself up the canyon walls, but he forced himself to focus on carefully planting his feet, on maneuvering on the ropes, wanting to hurry but not letting himself.

He stumbled and almost fell as he climbed onto the canyon rim. Jake steadied him and helped him up.

"I sent the others back to headquarters," Jake said. "I told them I'd wait for you. Gage and Deputy Prentice got called away to a burglary, but they reopened the road."

"Are Rosa and the baby okay?" Danny asked.

"Mother and baby made it up top safely and are on the way to St. Joseph's," Jake said. "Dad regained consciousness before the ambulance left and he should be able to meet them at the hospital."

Carrie unclipped herself from her climbing ropes and joined him. "I'll give you both a ride back to headquarters as soon as we get the gear packed," she said.

The three of them coiled ropes and organized equipment and lugged it to the back of her SUV. "I'll get the car started and let it be warming up," she said. She took out her keys and started toward the front of the vehicle, but halfway there, she stopped and let out a cry.

"What is it?" Danny hurried to her side.

She shook her head, lips pressed tightly together and pointed toward the ground.

Jake joined them. "Someone slashed your tires," he said.

Danny stared at the deflated tires, gashes visible in the sidewalls of both front tires. It took a sharp blade and real force to make a cut like that. Force with anger behind it—the kind of hatred that motivated a killer, even.

Chapter Eight

Jake radioed the sheriff's department while Carrie waited with Danny beside her car. Those gashes in her tires had been such a shock. There was something so violent—so mean—about them. She hugged her arms across her chest and tried not to look at them, but they pulled at her gaze. It was too dark without her headlamp to see much, but just knowing they were there frightened her.

"Are you okay?" Danny asked. He stood very close, not touching her but his warmth and bulk comforting all the same.

Jake joined them. "Someone will be along soon." He frowned at the ruined tires. "I was up here the whole time, since we arrived, and I never saw anyone near your car who wasn't supposed to be."

"Everyone would have been in and out of it, getting equipment," Danny said. "I don't see how a stranger could have gotten near it."

"Not to mention Gage and Dwight were here, directing traffic. And the ambulance with the paramedics was here, too."

"One of the team could have done it." Carrie hated saying the words out loud, but there was no sense pretending they weren't true. No one would have thought twice about a fellow team member hanging out around her car, and they all carried sharp knives to cut ropes or seat belts or even tree branches that got in their way.

"Let's see what Gage has to say," Jake said. "He said he would leave Dwight to take the burglary call and come back here to deal with this."

Fifteen long minutes later, Gage pulled in behind Carrie's SUV. He left his sheriff's department's SUV running, its headlights flooding the area with harsh white light. "You okay?" he asked Carrie.

She nodded, and he moved on to examine the damage to her tires. He listened to Jake's brief explanation and studied the car, then returned to Carrie. "Has anyone threatened you?" he asked.

"No."

"Have you argued with anyone—a coworker? Your ex-husband?"

"No."

"Ted was pretty upset with you the other night," Danny said.

They all turned to look at him. He flushed. "Not that I think Ted would so something like this," he said.

"What was the argument about?" Gage asked.

"He couldn't keep up when we were jogging up a trail in search of a lost hiker," Carrie said. "I sent him back down. He was upset, but he had left by the time I got back to the trailhead and I haven't spoken to him since."

"Ted wasn't here tonight," Jake said.

"Who was here?" Gage asked.

Carrie listed everyone who was present, and Jake added the names of the two paramedics. Gage wrote them all down. "Even if we found fingerprints on the vehicle, they could have been made by a team member who had a legitimate reason to be here," he said. "The mud is all trampled down with no distinct shoe impressions. I'll have someone take a look at the tires, see if they can figure out what cut them, but I'm not holding my breath that's going to help us."

"I can take you home," Jake said.

"Take us back to search and rescue headquarters and I'll take Carrie home from there," Danny said. "If that's okay with you?"

"Sure," she said. At least she wouldn't have to make polite conversation with Danny all the way home, the way she would feel the need to do so with Jake. They were comfortable enough with each other for silence.

"We have to get the search and rescue gear out of my car first," she said. "If we get another callout, we might need it."

They filled the back seat of Jake's SUV with climbing and medical equipment, then unloaded it all at SAR headquarters. Carrie sent Jake home and she and Danny put everything away, working silently, each knowing what to do without direction.

When they were done, she took one last look

around the room. "I guess that's all we can do for now," she said.

"Are you going to be okay?" he asked.

"My tires were slashed," she said. "That feels more petty than personal, at least right now."

"So you think this is related to the other attacks on search and rescue?" he asked.

"Don't you? Other than Ted, no one is angry with me, and we know Ted wasn't at the accident site tonight. There were too many people around who know him." She shook her head. "I think my car was there and it was an easy target for whoever is carrying this grudge against SAR. And the very worst thing is knowing it's probably one of us."

"I can't think of anyone in the group who's ever said anything against us," Danny said. "Yeah, Ted is upset right now, but he helped found the group. I can't believe he would ever try to destroy it."

"We know Ted didn't slash my tires, and I know it wasn't you." She fished her keys from her pocket and held them, more for something to do with her hands than anything else. "You were down in the canyon from the first tonight. You were descending into the canyon beside Tony when he was hurt. Maybe you could have put that acid on the ropes, but then why be the one to point it out when none of the rest of us had noticed? And you were with me when the Beast was set on fire, and here when Austen was run off the road."

"We don't know Austen's accident was related to the other incidents," Danny said.

"Right." She leaned against the table at the front of the room. "I don't think Jake is responsible, either. He wasn't present for any of the other incidents before tonight."

"Sheri was out of town tonight," Danny said. "At least she said she was and we don't have any reason to doubt that. She knows more than any of us about climbing, so she might have heard that acid could damage ropes without it being noticeable."

"Sheri has had friends in the climbing community who died in accidents," Carrie said. "I can't see her deliberately arranging for someone else to be injured. And she likes Tony. She likes everyone."

"Hannah was sick tonight, but I suppose she could have faked that and sneaked over to the canyon. Anyone who saw her would think she was supposed to be there."

"Except she and Jake are engaged and he would have noticed her and known she was supposed to be home with the flu. And again, Hannah is a paramedic. Maybe I'm naive, but I can't see her deliberately hurting anyone."

"No one has a motive that I can see," Danny said. "Ryan gets along with everybody and so does Eldon. Search and rescue saved Austen's life and he's the most dedicated volunteer we've had in years."

"Yeah, and when Austen doesn't like something, he doesn't keep his opinion to himself," Carrie said. "His complaints annoy me sometimes, but now I can see that he gets things off his chest and moves on.

I think we're looking for someone who is nursing a grudge we know nothing about." She stifled a yawn.

"We should get home." Danny suppressed a yawn of his own. "It's been a long day, and we aren't getting anywhere debating everyone's guilt or innocence."

"Yes, let's go." She straightened. She wanted to see her kids and her mom to reassure herself that they were all right. She seldom worried about her own safety, but the thought of anyone harming her family chilled her to the core.

Danny drove her through the silent town. Even Mo's Pub was closed now, the neon from its sign reflecting on the dirty snow banked alongside the street. He pulled his Honda to the curb in front of her house and shut off the engine. "I'll walk you to the door," he said.

"You don't have to do that,"

"Humor me."

She was aware of him looking around them, as if watching for trouble. "You're making me nervous," she said.

"Sorry." He shoved his hands in his pockets. "I didn't want to take any chances."

She stopped at the bottom of the steps. "My mom will still be up," she said. "I'll be fine. Thanks for the lift."

"No problem." He hesitated, then pulled her close in a hug. His arms tightened around her as she leaned into him. The embrace felt so good. Safe and…right.

She tilted her head to look up at him, to tell him thank you again. Her attention was caught by the glint of light on the stubble across his jaw and the deep laugh lines on either side of eyes with purple shadows beneath them. She had forgotten that he had worked a full twelve hours today before coming out into the cold to rescue two strangers. "You were great, delivering that baby tonight," she said. "I never would have guessed you were nervous if you hadn't told me."

"You were the one who was great," he said. "Calming the mom down and telling her what to do."

"She would have figured it out," she said. She smiled, remembering the sight of that tiny infant cradled in Danny's gloved hands. "It was a beautiful baby."

"Yeah." His gaze met hers and held, and she felt the pull of it, drawing her toward him. She tilted her head up farther and focused on his lips. They looked soft, and she wondered what they would feel like against hers. It had been so long since a man had kissed her. So long since she had even wanted that. But she wanted it now. She wanted Danny to kiss her.

The porch light suddenly bathed them in a harsh white glare and Carrie squeezed her eyes shut and silently cursed her mother's timing. "Carrie? Why are you standing out in the cold?"

Danny took his arms from around her and stepped back as they heard the locks on the door disengage. "I'd better go," he said, and headed down the walk, long strides carrying him quickly to his car.

"Carrie?" Her mom looked out the door. "Who is that with you?"

"That was Danny." She climbed the steps and

moved past her mother inside. "He gave me a ride home."

"Where is your car?" Becky asked. "Were you in an accident? Are you all right?"

"I'm fine. The car is fine, too." Or it would be, after she acquired two new tires.

"What's wrong? Why did Danny bring you home?"

"It's a long story. Let's make some tea and I'll fill you in." She would tell her mother almost everything. Except how Carrie was growing closer and closer to Danny Irwin—a man she had no business getting involved with. Danny was a fun, no-commitment kind of guy, but Carrie wasn't good at fun and frivolous. When she gave her heart, she went all-in. It was a bad habit she couldn't seem to break.

FRIDAY MORNING, Sheri called and invited Carrie to lunch. "Hannah is coming, too," she said. "She's feeling better and we want the scoop on what happened Wednesday night."

"It was no big deal," Carrie said. "We don't even know if it's related to everything else that has been happening."

"We're the only women with search and rescue," Sheri said. "We need to stick together. So let's have lunch and see what we can come up with if we put our heads together."

"Good idea." Carrie ended the call, feeling better than she had in weeks. She was pretty sure Hannah and Sheri didn't have anything to do with the attacks on SAR. And they were smart women with a lot of experience with search and rescue. Maybe they had realized something she hadn't, and together they could at least come up with some observations to share with the sheriff's department.

They met at eleven thirty at Kate's Kitchen, a short walk from Carrie's office. "It's my off period and then I have an hour that's supposed to be free to meet with parents, only I don't have anything scheduled," Sheri explained. She taught at Eagle Mountain High School.

"And I'm off all afternoon," Hannah said. She was a paramedic, and she helped her parents operate the Alpiner Inn.

"I've got two hours free, if one of you will give me a lift to Butch's garage to pick up my car," Carrie said. Butch had called to let her know he had set her up with new tires.

"I'll take you," Hannah said.

They chose a booth near the back and ordered salads and iced tea, then Sheri leaned across the table toward Carrie. "We want to hear everything," she said.

"Not just about your tires," Hannah added. "I heard you and Danny delivered a baby."

"A little boy," Carrie grinned. The magic of those intense moments in the canyon still lingered. "Mom and baby—and Dad, too—are all doing well. The dad had a concussion, but seat belts and airbags, and the fact that their van slid and never rolled over completely before it landed on that ledge, saved them all."

"Details, please," Sheri said.

Carrie took them through the events of the night, from the call from the emergency dispatcher to the moment when she, Danny and Jake discovered her tires had been slashed.

"Jake told me it took a big knife and a lot of force to cut those tires," Hannah said. The server had delivered their orders and she stabbed at a piece of romaine.

"Jake was up top, not far from where we had parked, the whole time," Carrie said. "He and the paramedics and Gage Walker and Dwight Prentice all say no one went near my car except the search and rescue volunteers who were unloading gear."

"Could someone have cut the tires back at your house or at SAR headquarters and it took a while for them to deflate?" Sheri asked.

Carrie shook her head. "These were big gashes. The tires would have deflated right away. No way could I have driven even a few yards without noticing."

"So what do they think happened?" Sheri asked. "One of the volunteers who was there that night just crouched down, stabbed your tires and no one else noticed?" She scooped up a forkful of quinoa and arugula and frowned, as if the salad was guilty of some offense.

"I guess so," Carrie said. "It doesn't make sense to me. I mean, do you two think any of our volunteers would do something like that?"

"Until recently, I would have said no way," Sheri said. "But Ted is really angry with all of us right now. I saw him in the grocery store yesterday and he headed in the opposite direction as soon as he spotted me. He's never acted like that before."

"Ted wasn't there Wednesday night," Carrie said. "And I don't see how he could have showed up without someone spotting him."

"What does Danny think?" Hannah asked.

The mention of Danny startled Carrie. Had the other women picked up on Carrie's attraction to the man? That would be beyond embarrassing. "Danny?" she asked, hoping she sounded more curious than concerned.

"That's right," Sheri said. "Since you and Danny were delivering a baby when your tires were ruined, he couldn't have been responsible."

"And he was with you when the Jeep was set on fire," Hannah said. "Besides, Danny doesn't have a mean bone in his body and he loves search and rescue. It's just about the only thing he's serious about."

"You two dated for quite a while, didn't you?" Carrie asked. She had been dying to find out more about Hannah's relationship with Danny, and this seemed like the perfect opportunity to slip it into conversation.

"Five months," Hannah said. "He's a sweet guy and pretty much the perfect boyfriend, as long as you're not looking for serious commitment. I was, so we agreed to break it off. And then I met Jake." Her eyes took on a dreamy expression at the mention of her fiancé.

"Danny and I dated a couple of times, too," Sheri said. "But he said I intimidated him. He kind of made it into a joke. The thing about Danny, he doesn't really want to be challenged. If he had a motto, it would be No Stress, No Mess. I think it's why he's so good at rescue work. He never gets too excited about anything. He's the most Zen guy I ever met, but frankly, I like a little bit more adrenaline in my relationships."

"Is that why you married a cop?" Hannah asked.

"And why I remarried him." Sheri laughed. She had recently gotten back together with her ex-husband, Detective Erik Lester, when they reconnected during the search for a missing child in Eagle Mountain.

"So what does Mr. Zen think about whoever is going after SAR members?" Hannah asked.

"He's as baffled as I am," Carrie said. "Jake, Austen, Eldon and Ryan worked that accident with us on Wednesday and none of them have given any indication they aren't really happy with the group."

"Ryan was out for a while after that fall off Mount Baker earlier this year," Sheri said. "But he seems to be in a good place. He told me he plans to return to climbing competitively as soon as possible."

"Eldon always complains about the cold," Hannah said. "But he's from Hawaii. I think he mainly does it to remind everyone he's from the islands, when secretly he loves it. He's out with his snowboard every chance he gets."

"Austen always gets annoyed when we have to rescue people who get in trouble because of their own carelessness," Carrie said. "But I think we all resent that sometimes."

"Sure, but we rescue them anyway," Sheri said. "We're not about judging."

"I think he's getting better about his attitude," Hannah said. "He's really dedicated."

"He is," Carrie said. "We all are. We couldn't do this work if we weren't."

They turned their attention to their salads, and no one said much for a while. Then Sheri said, "Maybe we're looking at this all wrong. Maybe the person who's doing this isn't angry with SAR. They could be upset on the organization's behalf."

"What do you mean?" Carrie asked.

"Look at the things they've done." She held up a hand and began counting off on her fingers. "They put acid on the climbing ropes. Maybe they didn't intend for anyone to be hurt. Maybe they thought we would notice before anything bad happened. Maybe they did it to call attention to our need for more money to update our equipment."

"That's a pretty indirect way to go about it," Hannah said.

"Yeah, but hear me out," Sheri said. "Next, they burn the Beast. That was a huge loss to the group, but in our heart of hearts, were any of us really sorry to see the old thing go? It has been nothing but trouble in recent months. Something always needs fixing, it drinks gas and it's no fun to drive. By destroying it, the arsonist forces us to find a way to get a new vehicle."

"Okay, but what about the attack on Austen and slashing my tires?" Carrie asked.

"Maybe attacking Austen was just a way to keep our attention," Sheri said. "Or maybe it wasn't connected to the other incidents. Maybe it really was a careless driver. And by slashing your tires, our attacker calls attention once again to the need for a new search and rescue vehicle."

"It's a really twisted, mean way to lobby for a new vehicle and new equipment," Hannah said.

Sheri shrugged. "It's just another way to look at things."

"How are our fundraising efforts going?" Carrie asked, ready to change the subject.

"The *Eagle Mountain Examiner* has agreed to run an article about our need for donations," Sheri said. "We're going to have a booth at next week's Spring Carnival and sell T-shirts and solicit donations. Austen and Eldon are helping me and they have some good ideas. And the county has agreed to match the first $10,000 we raise."

"I'm going to ask Tony to come up with some specs for a new vehicle," Carrie said. "I wanted Ted to work with him, but I don't know now if that will happen."

"Give Ted a little time to calm down," Sheri said. "I think he'll come around."

"Can I get you ladies anything else?" Their server stood by the table.

Carrie checked the time. "No thanks. I need to get back to the office." Time to focus on those drawings—one of the few things in her life she could control.

Chapter Nine

Danny worked ski patrol Saturday morning, so was late to the regular search and rescue meeting that afternoon. As Carrie called the meeting to order, he settled into a folding chair at the back of the room and studied his fellow volunteers. Could one of these people, all of whom he had literally trusted with his life at one time or another, really be set on hurting this organization that had helped so many people over the years? He dismissed each person in turn. She would never hurt anyone, especially not a fellow team member, and he was devoted to the group and the last person in the world Danny would expect to resort to violence.

By the time Carrie moved to the front of the room to begin the meeting, everyone had assembled, except Tony, who had moved to a rehab facility to continue his recovery, and Ted, who Danny was beginning to believe had left the group for good.

"Let's get started, everyone," Carrie said, and the murmur of conversation slowly died out.

Danny thought she looked a little more tense than

usual, a little paler, but maybe he was only projecting his own worries on to her. Seeing her tires slashed like that had really shaken him, as if for the first time he had realized they were all in danger.

"First up is a reminder about the course, Ground Search Awareness, hosted by Colorado search and rescue June 25," Carrie said. "Jake and Austen, you should definitely sign up for this, but it's a good refresher for everyone." She checked the notebook in front of her. "We also received a flyer from San Miguel County about a multiday course, Wilderness First Responder, they have planned for this summer, so be on the lookout for more information about that."

The side door opened and they all turned to look as Tony, leg outstretched in a wheelchair fitted for the purpose, rolled into the building, the chair pushed by Ted. "I figured I'd better show up to keep you all in line," Tony said.

Cries of surprise and welcome rang out as everyone rushed to greet the two new arrivals. "I called Ted and talked him into breaking me out of rehab for a couple of hours," Tony said as he shook hands and accepted pats on the back from everyone as Ted stood behind him, beaming.

Leave it to Tony to figure out a way to bring Ted back into the fold, Danny thought. The two might have argued in the past about Ted's role with the organization, but the older man wasn't the type to let down anyone who needed his help, especially someone like Tony, whom Ted had mentored as he came up through the organization.

"I didn't mean to interrupt," Tony told Carrie when some of the excitement over his arrival died down. "It took a little longer to maneuver this chair into the van Ted borrowed than we thought it would."

"That's okay," Carrie said. "It's great to see you." She smiled at Ted. "Both of you."

"Get back to conducting the meeting," Tony said. "I don't want to horn in."

"At the speed you're recovering, you'll be ready to teach that wilderness-first-responder class by summer," Ryan said.

Tony waved away the comment. "What's next on the agenda, Carrie?"

She glanced at her notebook. "Don't forget the search and rescue booth at next week's Spring Carnival," she said. "There's a sign-up sheet for everyone to take a shift. Anything you want to add about that, Sheri?"

"We got a new order of T-shirts in today—all sizes," Sheri said. "So tell your friends and relatives they all need one."

"Should have ordered sweatshirts," Ted said. "If it's like most spring carnivals, it will probably snow."

"It may say spring on the calendar, but not in Eagle Mountain," Hannah said.

"Snow is spring around here," Eldon said. "It's just wetter snow and you can ski in shirtsleeves."

"Any other fundraising news?" Carrie asked.

"Tammy Patterson with the *Eagle Mountain Examiner* is going to be calling you for quotes for the article she's doing highlighting our need for a new

search and rescue vehicle, so just a heads-up," Sheri said. She turned to Austen. "I know she for sure wants to talk to you, since you are someone we rescued who became a volunteer."

"Sure," Austen said, "I can do that."

"That's about it for now," Sheri said. "Though if anyone else has a fabulous idea for how we can raise a whole bunch of money, really fast, let me know."

"Thanks, Sheri," Carrie said. "That's all I have for tonight."

"Wait a minute," Austen said. "Do you have an update on the attacks on SAR and our volunteers? I heard whoever this person is, they went after you."

"Someone went after Carrie?" Tony's voice rose over the others as everyone began talking at once.

"Someone slashed my tires," Carrie said. "That's not exactly a personal attack."

"When was this?" Ted asked.

"Wednesday night, after our rescue of the pregnant woman and her family," Carrie said. "She and her baby and her husband are all doing great, by the way. She called me at work yesterday to say thank you."

"Do the cops have any idea who did it?" Eldon asked.

"No," Carrie said. "All they could tell me was that the tires were slashed on the scene, with a big, sharp knife. There really isn't any evidence for them to trace, and apparently no one saw anybody suspicious near my car."

"There really isn't any kind of pattern to any of these things," Hannah said. "Tony was hurt when someone put acid on his climbing ropes. Then someone burned the Beast. Someone ran Austen off the road, and then Carrie's tires were slashed. It's so random."

"It's like whoever is doing this doesn't really plan," Eldon said. "He—or she—just sees an opportunity to do something to hurt one or all of us and takes it."

"There's one thing all these incidents have in common," Danny said.

The others stared at him. "What's that?" Sheri asked.

"The most likely suspect for all of them is one of us," he said.

"No!" Hannah protested.

"That can't be right," Eldon said.

"Why do you say that?" Tony posed this last question. He leaned forward in his wheelchair, frowning.

"No one else had access to our climbing ropes," Danny said. "Same with the keys to the Beast—they're kept in here, and someone took them and moved the Beast away from the building before they torched it. No one else really uses the road up to the headquarters building, which makes it unlikely anyone else ran Austen off the road. And everyone from the paramedics on the ambulance to a trio of sheriff's deputies say no one but SAR volunteers was anywhere near Carrie's car while it was parked on the side of the road Wednesday night."

This declaration brought another uproar from the room. But Danny wasn't sorry he had given voice to what they all had to be thinking. Despite their protests, he read the doubt on all their faces.

"What are we supposed to do now?" Ryan asked. "I know I haven't done anything wrong, but I'm not about to start pointing fingers at the rest of you. We can't help other people if we start doing that."

"I'm not saying we should accuse each other," Danny said. Even though, in a way, he had accused all of them. "I just think we all need to be extra careful."

"Like we hadn't already figured that out," Austen said.

Carrie moved over to stand beside Danny. "I'm as upset about this as all of you," she said. "But we need to remember that we have one really big thing in our favor."

"What's that?" Ted asked.

She paused to look at each of them. When her eyes met Danny's he felt the impact of that look. "We're a team," she said. "We're trained to work together and to take care of each other. If one person has turned against us, they're already outnumbered." Another pause as everyone digested this. "The group is always stronger than the individual. Whoever you are, you can try to pick us off but you can't defeat us all."

Danny studied the faces of the others in the room. Carrie's words made most of them sit up straighter, a new determination in their eyes. Some nodded in agreement. "She's right," Sheri said.

"You tell 'em, Carrie," Eldon said.

No one looked guilty or afraid. Did that mean the person who had made so much trouble wasn't one of them after all?

Or did it only mean the guilty person was very good at hiding their true feelings?

"CAN WE GET cotton candy?" Amber asked as she and Dylan skipped alongside Carrie on the way to the park where the Eagle Mountain Spring Carnival was being held. The week since the search and rescue meeting had been a quiet one, with no callouts and no more vandalism or other mischief. Maybe Carrie's speech about them all sticking together had made an impact. Or maybe all the attention was scaring off whoever was behind the mysterious misfortunes that had plagued the group.

In any case, she was going to focus on spending a fun morning with her kids, and doing her best during her shift at the search and rescue booth this afternoon to collect more donations toward the purchase of a new vehicle. In spite of Ted's predictions of snow the weather had turned almost balmy, with plenty of sunshine, and the first daffodils nodded their heads along the borders of the park.

"And I want to get my face painted," Dylan said. "A big bug, so people will think I have a tarantula or a scorpion crawling across my face."

"Cotton candy and face painting are definitely on the agenda," Carrie said. "But first I have to stop by the search and rescue booth."

"Mo-om," Dylan whined. "You don't have to go save someone today, do you?"

"I hope not," Carrie said. "I just want to check the volunteers have everything they need." Her own shift at the booth started at one, after her mom completed her volunteer stint with the Women's Club and could take over looking after the children.

A large banner across the front of the Eagle Mountain Search and Rescue booth proclaimed "Help Fund Our New Search and Rescue Vehicle! Donate Today!" in bright red letters. Below that, an assortment of search and rescue T-shirts swayed in the breeze, like bright cotton streamers or maybe oversize prayer flags. "How's it going?" she asked Hannah, who manned the booth with Jake, the engaged couple wearing matching green SAR T-shirts.

"We've only sold one shirt," Hannah said.

"But we've collected several donations." Jake held up the cardboard box designated for donations and shook it, change clinking inside.

"Let's hope there's more than coins in there." Danny spoke from directly behind Carrie. The sound of his voice sent a flutter through her chest and she turned to look, tilting her head up to meet his smile. He wore a bright yellow SAR shirt, one that, as it happened, matched her own.

"There's checks and bills in there, too," Jake said.

"You're not on duty today?" Danny asked Jake.

"I go on shift at eleven," Jake said. "My uniform is in the car."

"Do you rescue people, too?" Carrie looked down to see her son, head tilted way back to look up at Danny, who towered over him.

Danny crouched down so that he was eye level

with Dylan. "I do," he said. He jerked his thumb toward Carrie. "Are you with her?"

Dylan nodded. "She's my mom."

"This is Dylan." Carrie rested her hand on her son's shoulder. "And this is my daughter, Amber." She stroked the top of Amber's head. The little girl had moved in closer to lean on Carrie's legs, though she kept her gaze fixed on Danny.

"Hello Dylan and Amber. I'm Danny. I work with your mom on search and rescue."

"We're going to get our faces painted," Amber said.

"Yes, and we'd better go do that, hadn't we?" Carrie said. Not that she was anxious to get away from Danny, but she felt the children's impatience and their unasked questions. Lately, they were hyperaware whenever she was anywhere near a man. She didn't know if it was because they wanted her to date someone who might be a potential father—or they were afraid she would.

She glanced at Danny and immediately pushed away the thought. Danny Irwin was definitely not potential-father material.

He straightened. "Mind if I walk with you?" he asked.

"You can come with us," Amber said before Carrie could answer.

He fell into step beside them, relaxed, focused as much on the kids as on Carrie. Or maybe even more on the kids. "I'm going to get a bug painted on my face," Dylan said to Danny.

"Seriously?" Danny asked. "That's so cool."

"I think it's gross," Amber said.

"That's 'cause you're a girl," Danny said.

"No, it's because a bug on your face is gross."

Dylan grinned up at Danny, who grinned back, as if in silent celebration of successfully grossing out his sister. "Which do you think is scarier?" Dylan asked. "A tarantula or a spider?"

"They're both pretty scary," Danny said. "We once had a patient at the surgery center where I work who had to have surgery on his leg because he was bitten by a black widow spider and his leg started rotting around the bite."

"Are you a doctor?" Amber asked.

"No, I'm a nurse."

"Did the guy's leg really rot off?" Dylan asked.

"No, but he had to have a big chunk of his calf cut out."

Carrie and Amber exchanged looks of disgust, but Dylan hung on every word as Danny described the black widow spider and the damage from its venom.

At the face-painting booth, Carrie turned the kids over to a pair of high school cheerleaders. The girls were manning the booth to raise funds for a band trip to the Rose Bowl next year. "You certainly made an impression on my son," she said to Danny.

"Little boys like gross stuff like that," he said. "It's normal."

"So I've noticed. His favorite books are the *Captain Underpants* series."

Danny laughed. "I'd probably like them, too."

She turned to watch Dylan, who was apparently describing the *huuuuge* spider he wanted painted on his cheek. She smiled as he spread his hands wide.

"That was a great speech you gave at the meeting last week," Danny said. "The whole 'all of us against the one bad apple' thing. That was very moving."

She looked at him, wondering if he was mocking her. "Are you being sarcastic?"

"No, I mean it. It really turned the mood around. We stopped being afraid, or at least suspicious, of each other and started feeling like a team again."

The praise made her feel too warm, and she looked away. "Well, it's true. This is just one disgruntled person who doesn't even seem that focused," she said. "I mean, Tony being injured was terrible, and the fire was a huge blow, but since then everything has been so petty. Slashed tires? Really? It's getting harder for me to take this seriously."

"We don't want him doing anything worse."

"Well, no, but I wish he would make a mistake," she said. "I want him to do something to reveal his identity."

"That might be good, if he did it without hurting anyone else. Without hurting you."

She thought she must have imagined those words, and whipped her head around to face him again.

"Mom, look! I got the coolest black widow spider!" Dylan launched himself at her and she staggered back.

"Oh my gosh, that is a scary-looking spider," she said. The cheerleader had done a good job with the black widow spider crawling up one cheek toward Dylan's eye, a bright red hourglass glowing on its back.

"I pulled up a picture on my phone," the girl said. "It kind of creeped me out, painting it."

Dylan laughed with glee as Carrie paid for the artwork and included a generous tip.

Amber was next, a blue butterfly seeming to flutter on her cheek. "You look beautiful," Danny said, and Amber's cheeks pinked with pleasure.

"Do you like cotton candy?" Amber asked Danny.

"I do," he said.

"Then, you should come with us to get some."

He looked to Carrie. "Is that okay?"

"Sure." Though spending time with him that didn't relate to work still unsettled her, it wasn't necessarily in a bad way. They set off across the park. The festival was getting more crowded as the day lengthened, and there were lines at several of the booths, including the Elks Club refreshment tent. "Do you really like cotton candy?" Carrie asked as they waited to place their order.

"It's not my favorite, but it's not terrible," he said.

"No, it is terrible," she said. "Like eating sweetened fiberglass insulation."

He laughed. "I never thought of it that way, but I still like it."

He made a point to order a large cone of cotton candy—pink like Amber's. Carrie opted for a soft pretzel, while Dylan insisted on a strip of orange-and-white taffy half the length of his arm. Danny bit into his cotton candy and chewed thoughtfully. “Only a little like insulation,” he said. “But tastier.”

Amber giggled. “Do you really eat insulation?”

“I’m a bachelor,” he said. “I eat everything.”

“Let’s check out the games!” Dylan pointed toward a section of the park set aside for various game booths.

“All right.” They began walking in that direction. “When are you working the SAR booth?” she asked Danny.

“One p.m.”

Another jolt of sensation shot through her. Excitement? “The same time as me,” she said.

He grinned. “I may have arranged it that way.”

“Wh…why is that?” She hated that she stumbled over the question, like some nervous teenager, even though that was exactly how he made her feel.

“I like hanging out with you.” They passed a trash can and he tossed the half-eaten cotton candy into it. “I kind of thought you liked hanging out with me, too.”

“Yeah, I do.” Where was he going with this? She thought back to their almost kiss in front of her house last Wednesday night. Part of her really wanted to know where kissing him might lead, but the rest of her remembered Hannah’s warning that Danny definitely wasn’t interested in commitment. She had two kids. She couldn’t afford a fling.

“What do you want?”

The question startled her. She stared at him. “Huh?”

He gestured toward the chalkboard set up in front

of the games area. "You have to buy tickets for the games. Should we get a whole book, or just a few? My treat, but you know your kids best."

"You don't have to pay," she said.

He shrugged. "I was going to buy some anyway. I like to try my hand at the baseball throw and stuff like that."

They settled on splitting the cost of a whole booklet because, as he pointed out, that was cheaper than the same amount of tickets purchased separately. Then they spent the next hour trying their hand at knocking over plastic ducks with baseballs, tossing basketballs into hoops and watching Amber and Dylan try to knock themselves off a low beam by whacking at each other with pillows. The match ended in a draw, with both of them rolling around in a deep bed of wood chips, giggling.

From there it was back to the food booths, where they shared a lunch of hot dogs and curly fries at a picnic table under the shade of a towering cottonwood. They had just sat down with their orders when Danny's phone rang. He pulled it from the pocket of his jeans and frowned at the screen.

"Is everything okay?" Carrie asked.

"Yeah." But he continued to stare at the phone, the cheerful notes of the ringtone repeating.

"I don't mind if you answer it," she said. She stood. "I can move over to give you some privacy."

"It's okay. I'll call back later." He swiped to reject the call and tucked his phone away again. Then he picked up his hot dog and took a big bite—was he really so hungry or did he just not want to talk?

She kept glancing at him, but he didn't look her way. He sat hunched, drawn into himself. Who had called that had changed his whole demeanor so drastically?

At ten minutes to one, Becky texted to ask Carrie's location and arrived five minutes later, as everyone was finishing their meal, to take charge of the children. "Hello, Danny," she said, then turned a questioning look to Carrie.

"Hey, Becky," Danny said. He smiled, more his old self now, though Carrie still detected a shell of reserve.

Carrie made a show of checking her watch. "We'd better head over to the search and rescue booth," she said. She hugged each of the children, who were already showing signs of fatigue and overstimulation. "Be good for Grandma."

"Thanks for letting me hang out with you," Danny said, then offered a fist for each child to bump in return, which had them both grinning. The more delighted the two children were, the worse Carrie felt. *Don't get too attached,* she wanted to tell them. *He's not the type to stick around.*

But really, she might have been saying the words to herself.

"What's going on at the booth?" Danny asked as they drew nearer.

Carrie had been so lost in her thoughts that she had somehow failed to register the crowd milling around the search and rescue booth, including two uniformed sheriff's deputies. She and Danny broke into a jog. "What's happened?" Carrie asked a distraught-looking Sheri. Behind her, Austen spoke to Jake, his voice raised but his words indistinct in the clamor of the crowd.

"All the money we collected today," Sheri said. She waved a hand toward the counter where the cardboard box with its collage of search and rescue photos had sat. "It's gone. Someone just walked off with it. Who would do something like that?"

Chapter Ten

"The donation box was in the open, right by the counter," Jake said. He was in his khaki sheriff's department uniform now and had apparently responded to the report of the theft, along with Deputy Wes Landry. "Anyone could have walked off with the box."

"But we were watching it," Sheri said. "If someone had leaned over the table to get it, I know I would have seen them."

"When was the last time you know for sure the box was there?" Wes asked.

"A man who said he was from Texas bought a T-shirt and put an extra twenty in the donation box," Austen said. "I thanked him."

"When was that?" Wes asked.

"I don't know for sure." Austen rubbed the back of his neck. "Maybe fifteen minutes before Sheri noticed the box was missing."

"I remember the Texan," Sheri said. "I'm sure I saw the box after he left." She bit her lip. "I had my back to it for a few minutes while I talked to a couple of my students who stopped to say hello, but I'm sure

I would have noticed if someone had leaned past me, into the booth."

"What did the box look like?" Wes asked.

"It's about eight inches square, with pictures from search and rescue training exercises pasted all over," Jake said.

"Hannah's mom made the box for us a few years ago," Sheri said.

"We have it out every time we do a booth like this," Carrie said. "No one has ever bothered it before."

"But everyone would know the box had money in it," Jake said. "That's all the provocation some people need."

"How much was in the box?" Danny asked. "Any idea?"

"I don't know exactly," Sheri said. "But people were being really generous. The Texan wasn't the only one who left a twenty. I'm thinking at least a couple hundred dollars."

"I bet it was more than that," Austen said. "Maybe three hundred."

Danny may have been the only one to hear Carrie's low moan. "What are our chances of getting the money back?" she asked Jake.

Jake shook his head. "That money is probably long gone by now, but we'll do a search of the area. Maybe the thief still has the box."

"I'll help look," Sheri said. She looked to Carrie. "You and Danny are here to take over the booth, right?"

"Sure," Carrie said. "You go do whatever you need to do."

"I'll come with you," Austen said. He followed her out of the booth.

Carrie looked a little dazed. Danny glanced around them. Now that the sheriff's deputies had moved away, no one was paying much attention. Word of the robbery hadn't spread yet and they had the next two hours of their shift manning the booth to get through.

"We need something else to collect donations in," he said. He dug around in a pile of plastic bins at the back of the booth. Amid a stack of volunteer sign-up sheets, old climbing rope and miscellaneous first aid supplies he found a battered climbing helmet. "This should work," he said.

A further search unearthed a black marker. He wrote Donations in sloppy printing around the opening of the helmet and set it on the table at the front of the booth. He studied it a moment, then pulled out his wallet and extracted a five-dollar bill and added this to the empty helmet. "I hear it's good to prime the pump, so to speak," he said. "Give people the idea."

She nodded and began straightening the stacks of folded T-shirts on the table. "Do you really think this was just some random thief?" she asked. "Or was it the person who's been harassing us for the past few weeks?"

"I think someone saw a chance for quick cash and took it," Danny said. "The money from the T-shirt sales wasn't touched." He picked up the bank bag tucked into a box of garments on the floor between them and unzipped it. "There's a couple hundred in here, easy. Anyone with SAR would know about the bag and where it's kept."

She nodded but didn't look convinced. "It seems like too big a coincidence for these things to keep happening by accident."

A couple approached and asked about search and rescue, and Carrie moved over to talk to them. Danny joined her a few minutes later when someone asked about the shirts. After that, they spoke with a steady stream of people. Before he knew it, his two-hour shift at the booth was more than half over.

"That helmet is filling up," Carrie said, peering into their new donation bucket. "Maybe we should take out everything but a couple of smaller bills—just in case our thief makes another try."

"Good idea." Danny pulled out a handful of cash and began smoothing out the bills and laying them out in the table, sorted by denomination.

But before he was finished, shouting drew his attention.

"What is going on?" Carrie was already moving out of the booth, toward Austen and Sheri, who were shouting at a third person. Danny shifted over until he could see that the target of their wrath was Ted. And was that their donation box he was carrying?

Ted pushed past Austen and Sheri and set the box on the table in front of Danny and Carrie, who had moved back into the booth. "And before you ask, it's empty," Ted said.

Carrie stared at the box. "Where did you find it?" she asked.

"In the trash in the men's room. It was just sitting on top."

"I told him he should have left the box where it was and called the sheriff's office," Sheri said. "If there were any fingerprints, they're gone now."

"Maybe he wanted those fingerprints gone," Austen said. "Or he wanted an excuse for his own prints to be on there."

"I didn't know why the box was there until you told me someone had taken it," Ted said. "And by that time I was already halfway back to here." He scowled at Austen. "As for you—if you're accusing me of something, come out and say it to my face."

Austen folded his arms across his chest and glared at Ted. "It just seems mighty convenient that you just happened to find that box, when we all know you've got a grudge against search and rescue because you're not up to the challenges of the work anymore."

"I'm in better shape than you'll ever be." Ted lunged for Austen, but Danny intervened, pulling the older man back. "It's true," Austen addressed Carrie. "Ted could have pulled off every one of the accidents that have happened to us so far."

"He couldn't have taken this box right from under our noses," Sheri said. "We know Ted. We would have spotted him long before he reached the booth."

"Maybe he waited until we were distracted," Austen said. "We should search him. He might have the money still on him."

Ted let out a roar of rage and lunged for Austen

again. This time it took both Danny and Sheri to hold him back.

"Stop it!" Carrie shouted.

Everyone fell silent, gaping at the woman who was, after all, their captain. Danny couldn't remember her ever losing her temper or even raising her voice, but right now her cheeks were flushed and she looked angry enough to spit nails. "No one is going to search anyone," she said. "If whoever is targeting SAR wants to destroy us, they're doing so by getting us to argue like this."

The others looked appropriately sheepish, though Ted and Austen continued to watch each other out of the corners of their eyes, like battling dogs circling one another.

"I'll get in touch with the sheriff's office and let them know we found it." Sheri took out her phone.

"I'm sorry if I messed up any evidence," Ted said. "I thought maybe the box had been thrown away because the bottom was busted out." He turned it over to show how it had been torn almost completely off. "I brought it back here to ask what had happened and to suggest that instead of just tossing it, we might try to repair it." He shook his head. "I remember when Brit made that box for us. She put a lot of work into it."

"It's okay." Carrie patted his shoulder.

"Whoever took the box probably tore it open to take the money." Danny picked it up and examined the damage. "It doesn't look cut or anything, just ripped open."

"It's just cardboard," Ted said. "Easy enough to tear with a little effort."

"Maybe we can tape it back up and keep it at the station as a memento," Carrie said. "We'll let the sheriff's deputies look at it, but I don't think it's going to help them find who did this. I think the money is just gone."

Sheri ended her call. "Jake says he'll stop by and collect the box. They still might find some prints that don't belong to one of us." She turned to Ted. "I'm sorry I went off on you like that. I overreacted."

"It's okay," Ted said. "At least you didn't accuse me of stealing from SAR." He looked around. "Where's Austen?"

"He left," Danny said, "probably because he didn't want to face you." Austen had looked almost furtive, slipping away while everyone else was focused on the box. He had likely realized how out of line he had been to accuse Ted. Sure, Ted had had an opportunity to put acid on the climbing ropes or burn the Jeep, but why would he? Ted might be afraid of losing his role in SAR, but he would never destroy it. The organization was too much a part of his identity.

The others left when a trio of women approached and asked about purchasing T-shirts. Jake arrived and took charge of the box. "We probably won't find anything useful," he said. "But we'll see if we can lift some prints, and we can ask if anyone saw a man going into that restroom with it."

At three o'clock Eldon arrived, followed by Ryan, and Carrie filled them in on this latest development.

"We've been emptying the helmet every so often to keep the funds from building up too much," Danny said. "There's an envelope in the bank bag marked Donations, where you can put anything you collect."

"I think that's my old helmet," Ryan said. He pointed to a Patagonia sticker on the side and a large scuff in the surface. "From when that serial killer, Charlie Cutler, pushed me of Mount Baker. I had to retire it after that."

"It makes a cool donation bucket," Eldon said. "Especially when it's not empty, like your head." He laughed and dodged away from Ryan.

"Just keep a close eye on that money and bring everything to the station when you're done." The booths would shut down at five, when the light began to fade and temperatures turned cooler.

Danny walked with Carrie toward the parking lot. "What are your plans this afternoon?" he asked.

"Mom texted that she took the kids home about an hour ago," she said. "I plan to take it easy with them. What about you? Do you have a hot date?"

"No." The answer surprised him a little. He seldom spent a weekend without some female companionship. He had a list of women he could count on for a fun evening, even at short notice. He started to say he might call someone and go out, but stopped himself. He really didn't want to see one of those women. "I really had a good time with you and your kids today," he said.

"Oh. I had a good time, too." Her cheeks flushed and she jiggled her keys, as if suddenly nervous.

Her car lights flashed and he realized they were almost to her SUV. She stiffened as she looked toward it. “What is Austen doing by my car?” she asked.

“Hey, Carrie.” Austen, who had been leaning against the side of her SUV, straightened. He glanced at Danny, then turned his attention back to Carrie. “I wanted to apologize for losing my temper with Ted,” he said. “I was just so upset about that missing money. And I guess I feel guilty because that box disappeared while I was helping with the booth.”

“You should talk to Ted,” Carrie said.

“I will,” Austen said. “But I didn’t want to leave with you thinking bad of me.”

“I don’t think bad of you,” she said.

She moved closer to the SUV, as if she wanted to get in, but Austen didn’t move away. “What you said earlier, about all the things this person is doing tearing us apart, do you think that’s true?” he asked.

“It could be, if we don’t pull together more,” she said.

“But losing that money is just a little setback,” Austen said. “It won’t take us down.”

“No, it won’t,” Carrie said.

Austen studied the ground between his feet. Danny leaned forward, ready to suggest he move over so Carrie could go home to her family. That was what she really wanted. She didn’t want to be here with either of them.

“Are you afraid?” Austen asked.

The question clearly surprised her. “Why would I be afraid?” she asked.

"This guy slashed your tires. And he tried to kill Tony. You're the captain now, so aren't you afraid he'll go after you?"

Was Austen trying to frighten Carrie, or was he too dense to understand the effect his words might have?

But Carrie's expression didn't change. "Whoever is doing this isn't powerful," she said. "He strikes me as more...pathetic."

"Pathetic?" Austen echoed.

"Yes. If the same person is responsible for all the things that have been happening to SAR, what he's been doing is so petty. Yes, Tony could have died from that acid on the ropes, but I'm not sure this guy didn't intend to just vandalize some equipment and things got out of hand. The Beast was a big loss, but we all know it was on its last legs. Since then everything's been schoolkid pranks—the equivalent of stealing lunch money and letting air out of bicycle tires. It's annoying, but silly, too. To me, that makes him pathetic, and we need to remember that." She touched his shoulder. "Go apologize to Ted and try not to worry about the money. I'll see you at the next SAR meeting if not before."

He stepped aside and she opened the door and got into her SUV.

"Maybe wait until tomorrow to talk to Ted, when he's had a chance to cool down," Danny said.

Austen scowled at him. "When I want your advice, I'll ask for it," he said, then stalked off before Danny could formulate a reply.

CARRIE GAVE HER mom credit for waiting until after dinner before she mentioned Danny. "I didn't realize you and Danny Irwin were such good friends," Becky said as Carrie helped her with the dishes. Amber and Dylan were in the other room watching television.

Carrie kept her expression neutral. "We work together on search and rescue," she said.

"Oh, I know that." Becky dropped a handful of silverware into the basket of the dishwasher with a sound like castanets. "But since when do the two of you spend the morning with the children—a regular family outing?"

"Mom!" Carrie sent a warning glance toward the living room. "It wasn't like that."

"The children seem to like him. He was all they talked about all afternoon. Amber even asked me if he was your boyfriend."

Carrie winced. "Danny isn't my boyfriend," she said. "We're just...work friends."

"There's nothing wrong with being more than work friends," Becky said.

"Mom, I don't want to have this discussion." She pushed in the chairs around the table. "And Danny isn't interested in me that way," she added.

"You mean romantically?" Becky asked. "Or sexually?"

"Mom!"

Becky laughed. "You know him better than I do, but you're an attractive young woman and he's a healthy young man. It usually doesn't take much more than that to get something started."

"I'm not interested in starting anything."

"So you say. I'm just not sure I believe you."

It wasn't a matter of belief, Carrie thought. She did find Danny attractive, and it mattered to her that Dylan and Amber liked him and he seemed to like them. But she had given her heart and had it handed back to her once already. She wasn't prepared to go through that again. Danny had never tried to deceive anyone about his nature—he liked relationships with low expectations. He was all about fun, not family. Carrie was the opposite—she wanted a love like her parents', one that lasted for a lifetime. Obviously, there were no guarantees in relationships, but the odds were better if both partners started out wanting permanence.

SHE WASN'T THINKING about permanence on Monday at work, when Greg Abernathy called her into his office. "Sit down, Carrie," he said, nodding to the chair across from his desk. His office was easily twice the size of Carrie's, with white carpeting and chrome and leather furniture that looked out of place in the old Victorian home. "I want to discuss the Cornerstone development."

Carrie sat up a little straighter. Cornerstone was a four-office complex being built on the site of a building that had burned last summer, on the edge of downtown. The developer, Miles Lindberg, had specifically requested Carrie as the architect. "I've gone over some preliminary drawings for Mr. Lindberg and he seems very pleased," she said. So much so that he was talking about doubling the size of the build.

Abernathy nodded, his expression grave. "That's good to hear. I've decided to bring Vance in on the project," he said. "I need you to bring him up to speed."

Vance Weatherby was an architect who had been hired a year after Carrie, an amiable man who struck her as of mediocre talent and low ambition. "Why are you bringing in Vance?" she asked. "I thought I was going to handle the project by myself."

"Since the customer has expanded the scope of the build, we thought it would be a good idea to bring in an additional person," Abernathy said. "And we want Vance to get more familiar with all our major clients. That kind of knowledge will be invaluable as he moves up the ladder at the company."

Up the ladder. Carrie translated this to *making partner*, something that had never been offered as a possibility to her, though she had hoped being given the Cornerstone project on her own had been a signal that the partners wanted to give her more responsibility. "I'd like to be more involved with all our clients, too," she said, and sat up a little straighter. "And I want to move up the ladder as well."

She couldn't figure out the look he was giving her right away, then she realized he was puzzled. "I thought you were happy with your role here," he said. "You made your feelings about the job clear when we hired you and we think your situation has worked out well."

"What situation is that?" she asked.

"From the first you indicated that what you wanted most from the job was the flexibility to devote time to your family," Abernathy said. "We've been happy to support that, even if it has made things difficult for us at the same time."

"I always complete my work on schedule," she said. "My clients have been very pleased."

"Oh, of course. But you've never really taken on anyone demanding. That's why we'd like Vance to work with you on the Cornerstone build. He'll have the time to devote to it." He stood. "Get with him this afternoon and bring him up to speed. That's all."

Half a dozen replies whirled through her head, most of them things she would probably regret saying, so she merely nodded and returned to her office. How much of what had just transpired was Abernathy's fault and how much her own, for putting her family ahead of her job? But she shouldn't ever have to regret that, should she?

She didn't have much time to stew over the matter. She had barely settled back at her desk when Vance leaned into her office. "Greg said you'd bring me up to speed on the Cornerstone project. He said with your busy schedule, you could use a hand."

Why did a remark that could have passed for concern sound so much like an insult? But she shoved aside her annoyance and invited Vance in to go over the particulars of what had, until a few moment ago, been her biggest solo effort to date.

Three hours later, jaw aching from forcing so many smiles and temper frayed to the point where she was sure at any moment she would say the exact wrong thing, she left the office. If her bosses were going to view her as a slacker because she set her schedule around her family's needs why not take full advantage of that freedom?

She had an unsettling feeling of déjà vu as she approached her car and recognized the man leaning against it. "Austen? What are you doing here?" she asked.

He swept a fall of light brown hair out of his eyes and grinned at her. He looked particularly boyish today, dressed in a fisherman's sweater and dark jeans, and loafers without socks. "I didn't want to bother you at work," he said. "But I was hoping I'd catch you when you came out."

"What do you want?" The words came out brusquer than she had intended, but really, she was so tired of dealing with people today. Austen probably had some complaint about SAR. Despite his rookie status, he liked to point out things he thought they were doing wrong.

Either he didn't pick up on her foul mood or he chose to ignore it. "I wanted to ask you out," he said. "For dinner. Friday night."

She didn't do a good job of hiding her shock. She openly stared at him. "You're asking me on a date?"

"Yes. I mean, why not?" He shoved his hands in the front pockets of his jeans, his smile fading. "We're both single, we're almost the same age and I think we have a lot in common." He raised his head, chin jutted out. "I'll admit I'm a little rusty. I haven't gone out with anyone since my fiancée was killed, but did I botch this so badly?"

She immediately felt terrible. Of course it hadn't been easy for him to ask her out, after the tragedy he had weathered. She managed a genuine smile. "I'm sorry. I'm really out of practice, too. I haven't dated anyone since my divorce, several years ago." Did that sound too pathetic?

He shifted his stance from one foot to the other. "I thought maybe you and Danny were involved."

She felt the heat rise to her cheeks. "No. We're not."

"Yeah, well, when I saw him at Mo's Saturday night, I figured maybe I was wrong."

"He was at Mo's with someone?" The thought pained her, though really, why should it? Danny was free to see whoever he pleased.

"He said he was waiting for someone. I figured it was a woman. He has a different one every time I see him."

Yes, that was the Danny she knew. Time to move on. "I'm flattered you asked me, Austen," she said. "But between my job and search and rescue and my kids, I don't have time to date. But if I change my mind, I'll let you know."

"Don't think of it as a date," he said. "Just friends getting together. It would really be nice not to have to eat alone."

Was he trying to guilt her into going out with him? "No, I really can't." she said. She hit the button to unlock her car and it beeped.

But Austen didn't move. As she tried to push past him, he grabbed her arm. "I wish you'd reconsider," he said. "I really do think we have a lot in common."

She pulled away, her earlier annoyance returning. "No," she said, and yanked open her car door, forcing him to move. She slid in and slammed the door behind her, then started the engine. Out of the corner of her eye she could see him standing there, glaring at her.

Let him glare. She was so over dealing with men today.

Chapter Eleven

The spring thaw brought warmer weather, the first wildflowers and spectacular waterfalls. It also delivered mudslides, floods and accidents involving people anxious to climb peaks and hike higher elevations before it was safe to do so.

On a Sunday afternoon a week after the Spring Carnival, search and rescue responded to a report of a car swept off the highway by a slide of rocks and mud, into a flood-swollen river.

“Word is there’s at least one person trapped in the vehicle,” Carrie informed the others gathered at SAR headquarters.

“I’ll get the Jaws,” Ryan said. The Hurst hydraulic extraction tool, better known as the Jaws of Life, was a powerful cutting tool designed to free a person from a wrecked vehicle.

“I’ll help,” Eldon said, and the two headed for the storage closet where the tool was kept.

Danny inventoried his medical pack, deciding if he needed to add anything to deal with the potential injuries. “Do we know how many people were in the vehicle?” he asked.

"The 9-1-1 caller said he thought five or six," Carrie said. Which could mean anything from two to ten. Danny added a few more cervical collars to his pack.

"I really miss the Beast," Sheri said as she hauled a litter out the side door. Larger equipment, like the litters, stayed packed in the rescue vehicle, ready to go without a volunteer having to remember to take it and figure out how to transport it. They were still short some items that had been burned along with the Beast.

"We can take my truck," Ted said. "A lot of equipment will fit in it."

"Thanks," Carrie said. She seemed to be making a point to welcome Ted back to the group, no questions asked.

"Carrie?" An agitated-looking Ryan approached their captain as she helped Austen stack coils of ropes in bins to be carried to a waiting vehicle. "Did someone move the Jaws?" he asked.

"The Jaws is in the closet, where it's always kept," she said.

"No, it isn't," Ryan said.

"We took everything out," Eldon said. "It's not there. And it's not like it's easy to overlook." The Jaws was over three feet long and weighed more than fifty pounds. Not to mention the blaze-orange reflective stripes across its case made it stand out even more.

Carrie and Austen followed them to the closet. Danny set aside the medical pack and joined them. The large space usually filled by the Jaws was empty.

"Do you think someone stole it?" Eldon asked.

"And did what with it?" Carrie asked. "It's not like you can sell something like that on the street."

"Maybe it's the same person who's been harassing us," Austen said.

"This is beyond harassment," Carrie said, her voice rising. "This could cost someone their life." She looked at all of them gathered around her. "We don't have time to deal with this now. We need to get moving. I'll call the sheriff and see if they can find an extractor we can use if the need arises. Get going."

They formed a caravan of four vehicles headed to the site of the mudslide, on a county road east of Eagle Mountain. Danny loaded into Carrie's car, along with Austen and most of their medical equipment. Jake and Sheri had the rest of the medical gear they might need, while Ryan, Ted and Eldon carried the climbing tools in Ted's truck.

Barricades stopped them just ahead of the ten-foot-wide river of orange mud that covered the road, rocks suspended in the muck like nuts in fudge.

Sheriff's deputy Wes Landry walked over to Carrie's car. "You'll have to park here and haul your equipment out to where the vehicle went over." He gestured toward the middle of the mud where Sgt. Gage Walker stood with Deputy Jamie Douglas. "It's a minivan, with two adults and four kids," Wes continued. "They're stuck on a rock outcropping on the far side of the river, which is running high."

"Is anyone in the vehicle?" Carrie asked.

"No. Everyone is out, but they aren't really dressed

for the weather. There are ice chunks floating in that water, not to mention tree trunks and other debris."

They climbed out of the SUV and stood at the edge of the mud flow, surveying the scene. The others joined them. "I wish I'd thought to bring muck boots," Sheri said.

"Nothing to do but wade through it," Ted said. He shouldered a coil of rope and started out, the mud rising above his ankles.

The others gathered equipment and followed, picking their way through the sludge and debris, every step making a sucking sound as they lifted their feet. The mud was cold and laden with sharp rocks that bit into Danny's ankles.

Thoughts of his own discomfort fled when they reached the shoulder of the road where Gage and Jamie stood and looked down into the river. Five people huddled together beside a crumpled van. A sixth person, a man, sat beside the van, head in his hands. Whitewater foamed around the rock, the roar of it drowning out all other sound.

"We're going to need to get a couple of people over to the other side to set up a traverse line." Sheri raised her voice to be heard above the thunder of the water. "Ryan, Ted, Carrie and I have taken the swift-water rescue course, so two of us should go."

"I'll go," Ted said.

Carrie shook her head. "No. Sheri and I will go. I want you here, as incident commander."

Ted glowered. "But I—"

"No arguments, Ted." She moved past him.

"All right," she continued. "Ryan, you and Austen set the line from this end. Danny, you get ready to go over on the traverse if they need medical assistance. Eldon, you and Jake help with the ropes."

"Where's Hannah?" Sheri asked.

"She's on shift with EMS today," Carrie said as she searched through the gear they had carried over for a helmet and life jacket. "She texted when the 9-1-1 call went out that she was on a run to the hospital in Junction and unavailable."

Sheri and Carrie donned helmets and life vests, then walked farther down the road to assess the situation, while Danny found a helmet and got into a harness, prepared to traverse down the rope line the others would set if any of the people in the canyon needed more medical attention than Carrie and Sheri could provide.

The women returned after ten minutes. "There's a couple of downed trees spanning the river farther downstream," Sheri said. "It looks like we can use them as a makeshift bridge to the other side and scramble down the shore to the outcropping where the family is stuck."

"If you fall in that water, you'll be swept away," Danny said. The idea made him a little queasy.

Carrie nodded. "Probably be sucked under, or caught on debris and drowned. So we won't fall in."

"It's a big risk," Danny said. He wanted to tell her she shouldn't go but figured she wouldn't listen to his objections and might even resist them. She was as well trained as any of them, he just hated the idea of her putting herself in danger. It was a new feeling for him, and he didn't especially like it, so he kept his mouth shut.

"Not that big a risk," Sheri said. "We can do it."

They roped up, in the hope that they might be pulled to safety if they did fall in. Danny stood with Ted and watched as first Sheri, then Carrie crawled out onto a massive cottonwood that lay on its side over the foaming water. Once on the trunk, Sheri stood and inched along to the jagged end and a gap of several feet they would have to clear to reach the second trunk, which formed the other half of the bridge.

Ted swore as Sheri made the leap to the second trunk. She turned and gave a thumbs-up signal, grinning widely, and Ted grumbled even more. "She's going to get in trouble, showing off like that," he said.

"You're just jealous you can't do it," Danny said.

"I'm too smart to take those kind of chances," Ted said. "You don't get to be my age by being foolish."

Sheri almost danced to the other side of the canyon and scrambled out onto the rocks and turned to watch Carrie complete the crossing. At the gap between the trees, Carrie hesitated. Danny could see Sheri's lips moving as she called to Carrie, but he couldn't make out her words from here.

Carrie nodded, gathered herself, then leaped. She hit the second trunk at an angle, and her back foot slipped into the water. Danny leaned forward, every muscle tensed as Carrie scrambled to right herself, then lost her balance and, arms flailing, fell backward into the water.

"No!" Danny shouted, and raced to where Ryan and the others waited with the ropes needed to rig a traverse line. He could hear Ted's feet pounding the ground behind him. Sheri had run back out onto the tree trunk and straddled it, both arms reaching for Carrie, who still clung to the trunk, most of her body in the frothing water.

"Someone should go help them," Austen said.

"Wait." Ted held up one hand and they all stared, no one making a sound as Carrie, with Sheri's help, hauled herself back onto the trunk. She lay there a long moment, water streaming from her body. "Is she okay?" Eldon asked.

"She'll be hypothermic if she doesn't get into dry clothes," Danny said. He cupped his hands to his mouth. "Carrie! Get back up here!"

Carrie pulled herself into a sitting position and looked back over her shoulder. "Come back!" Danny shouted again, and motioned for her to return to this side of the canyon.

Carrie stood and waved, but turned away, following Sheri to the opposite bank.

"I need to get down there and make sure she's okay," Danny said. He prepared to descend after the women, but Ted took hold of him.

"Wait for the traverse line," Ted said. "She looked like she's fine."

The two women picked their way along the opposite shore, moving along a narrow strip of slanted ground just above the water.

"Get ready to fire that rope across to the other side," Ryan said.

Eldon and Austen unpacked the line gun from its case. The gun used compressed air to send a projectile attached to stout rope across a distance of over two hundred yards, depending upon conditions.

Carrie and Sheri had reached the rock outcropping, and the family members crowded around them. Ted's radio crackled.

"We're ready to receive the line," Carrie said. "The driver of the car has a pretty bad head injury. I'd like Danny over here to assess him. A couple of the kids might be suffering from hypothermia, but we're going to get them wrapped up as warmly as we can."

"Roger that," Ted said.

Ten minutes later, with everyone standing well back from the target, Ryan fired the launcher and sent a ribbon of polypropylene unspooling across the narrow canyon. As soon as the projectile on the end struck the rock, Sheri was on it, fastening it to the anchor Carrie had already set. Eldon did the same on his end.

Danny moved into position and clipped onto the line, then rode down the line as if on a zip line. As he left, he heard Ted radioing for a couple of ambulances. Once on the other side, he moved to Carrie. "Are you all right?" he asked. "You must be freezing."

"I'm fine." She didn't even look at him, focused on wrapping a blanket around a child who looked like the youngest member of the party. "You need to look after

Mr. Hamilton." She nodded toward the dark-haired man who sat in the dirt beside the wrecked van.

Danny wanted to put his hands on her shoulders and look in her eyes for any signs of disorientation, to take her temperature and insist she change into dry clothing and drink something warm and take care of herself. Instead, he turned away to see to Hamilton, who showed signs of a serious concussion. "We need to get a medical helicopter on the way," Danny told Carrie when she joined him beside Hamilton. "And tell them to send over a litter to transport him."

While Carrie radioed this information to Ted, Danny and Sheri explained to the family how they were going to evacuate them. "Dad's going to go across first in this special litter," Sheri said. "Then the rest of you will ride over, kind of like being on a zip line, except we'll have people pulling you across on a pulley system. You'll be secured so you can't fall, and you'll all wear helmets and life jackets."

The two oldest children looked excited, Danny thought, while the youngest clung to mom, her thumb in her mouth. Mrs. Hamilton looked worried and exhausted. Danny couldn't blame her. As he helped get Mr. Hamilton secured into the sled, he kept sneaking glances at Carrie. She had to be freezing in her wet clothing, but she kept moving among the kids, wrapping them in blankets and helping fit them with helmets and life jackets.

Finally, they were ready to start across. The litter with Mr. Hamilton would go first, with Danny in line behind, holding on to it. They had learned the hard way that if someone didn't steady it, the litter could spin or twist, at worst tangling in the line and at best subjecting the occupant to a very uncomfortable ride. Carrie would come next with the youngest child, then the two older children and Mrs. Hamilton, and finally Sheri. Once everyone was taken care of, someone would repeat the river crossing Sheri and Carrie had made earlier, to unfasten the rope and retrieve the anchor.

The short trip across the narrow canyon took twenty uncomfortable minutes, with Danny steadying the litter until the muscles in both shoulders screamed for relief. He stumbled off the line onto solid ground and shook out his hands, then joined Ted in carrying Mr. Hamilton through the mud to the waiting ambulance, which would take it to the landing area a short distance away, where the medical helicopter was waiting.

Danny got back to the end of the traverse line in time to greet Carrie as she unhooked the youngest Hamilton child in her arms. Danny took the child from her. "Go get into some dry clothes," he said gruffly. "And don't pretend nothing is wrong. I can see you shaking, and your lips are blue."

She didn't even try to argue, which told him how much she was suffering. But he had to trust someone else would take care of her as he helped each of the children off the line and kept them together until they were reunited with their mother. "Is my husband going to be okay?" Mrs. Hamilton asked as soon as he handed off the youngest child to her.

"He's going to be on his way to the hospital soon,"

Danny said. "There are some paramedics waiting to check on you and your children, and then the sheriff's deputies will arrange for you to go to the hospital to see your husband."

"Is something wrong with my children?" she asked.

"It's just a precaution," Danny said. A couple of the children had showed indications of hypothermia when he had examined them after he first arrived in the canyon, but they were already showing signs of improvement. For the fourth time that day he trekked back through the mud, leading the family to the waiting ambulance and turning them over to the paramedics.

He returned to the canyon where the others were already in the process of collecting their gear. "Where's Carrie?" he asked.

Sheri looked up from the pile of life jackets she was packing back into a plastic tote. "I don't know. I haven't seen her for a while."

Danny looked around. Ted was helping to haul the traverse line back up from the canyon. "Ted! Where's Carrie?" he called.

Ted looked up, frowning. "I don't know," he said. "I'm sure she's around here somewhere."

Had she become disoriented with the cold and wandered off? Heart pounding, Danny ran along the edge of the canyon, searching. He asked each person he passed if they had seen Carrie. "Maybe she went back to her car," Eldon said. "She said something about getting out of her wet clothes."

Of course. That had to be it. Danny set out toward Carrie's SUV, but running was impossible in the mud, though a county crew with a front end loader had finally arrived and begun scraping up the muck so the road could reopen to traffic. He reached Carrie's SUV, but felt as if he had swallowed rocks when he saw that it was empty. He looked around, panic rising to choke him. Deputy Jamie Douglas waved to him from her sheriff's department cruiser and he headed toward her.

"Are you looking for Carrie?" Jamie asked. The slim dark-haired deputy was a familiar figure in town, currently the only woman on the force.

"I'm right here," Carrie said before he could answer.

He leaned down and relief flooded him as he spotted her in the passenger seat of the cruiser, a blanket around her shoulders and both hands wrapped around a steaming drink. "I figured the best thing was to warm her up fast, before she had to take an ambulance ride herself," Jamie said.

Jamie's radio crackled with a message that she needed to help with crowd control as they prepared to reopen the highway. "I need to go," she said.

"I'm good now." Carrie unwrapped the blanket from her shoulders and slid out of the cruiser. "Thanks," she told Jamie.

Jamie waved, climbed into the car and drove away. Carrie started to walk away, but Danny took hold of her arm. "Let me see," he said.

"I'm fine now. Really," she said.

He kept hold of her arm as he looked into her eyes, put the back of his hand to her cheek, then slid his fingers down to check the pulse at her throat. Her skin was satin soft and invitingly warm. He wanted to press his lips to that steady heartbeat just beneath her jaw, to lose himself in discovering every curve and velvety place on her body.

"Danny?" Her voice was scarcely above a whisper.

He pulled his mind away from the dangerous path it was taking, but he didn't lift his hand from her or shift his gaze away. "I don't think I've ever been so terrified as when I saw you go into the water," he said, his voice ragged.

"That makes two of us," she said, and tried to smile, but her bottom lip trembled, and he saw the flash of fear in her eyes as she relived the moment when the icy floodwaters had tried to claim her.

That trembling was his undoing. He bent and pressed his mouth to hers, stilling the tremor, pushing back the fear. She leaned into him, fingers clutching at his jacket, and he pulled her closer, as he had wanted to pull her from the water. He wanted to memorize the feel of her, to revel in the strength and softness and life in her.

She broke the kiss first but didn't pull away. "I'm okay, really," she said.

He nodded. "I know that now. But if anything had happened to you—"

"Shhh." She pressed fingertips to his lips and the gesture sent an electric current of desire through him. But this wasn't the time, or the place. He forced himself to release his hold on her and step back. Her cheeks were flushed, her eyes bright and she looked impossibly beautiful. "Just…don't do that again," he said.

She laughed. "I don't have any plans for it." She shoved her hands into the pockets of her parka. "You'd better go. I need to see that everything is wrapped up here."

"I can help," he said.

"Thanks, but I think it would be better if you go. Just for now." Her smile softened the words. "Okay?"

He nodded. "Yeah. Okay."

She turned and walked away and he tried not to focus on the sway of her hips, but he did. He wiped one hand across his face and took a deep breath, then turned around. Eldon was walking toward him, a coil of rope over each shoulder. "Can I catch a ride back with you?" Danny asked, taking one of loops from Eldon. "Carrie wants to finish things up here and I need to get back."

"Sure," he said. "I'm ready to go now."

He wasn't prepared to leave Carrie, but she was right—they needed the space. He still felt shaky from the impact of seeing her go into the water, and shocked by his own strong reaction to her brush with death. He had always liked not being closely tied to anyone else. Could his whole outlook on life really change with one slip of a foot?

Chapter Twelve

"The theft from our booth at the Spring Carnival set back our fundraising efforts," Sheri reported at the next search and rescue meeting, the following Saturday afternoon. "We ended up with about $500 for the day, most of that from generous people who heard about the theft."

"We're never going to reach our goal at that rate," Austen said.

"It's just a setback," Sheri said. "Eldon and Ryan and I have been working on some other ideas to bring in funds." She nodded to Ryan, who strode to the front of the room, a single sheet of paper in hand.

"We're sending a letter to all our past donors, asking them to make a special contribution toward a new rescue vehicle." Ryan held up the paper. "This is the letter, and we want everybody here to sign at the bottom. Then we'll scan it in and print off a bunch to mail out." He laid the letter on the front table and returned to his seat.

Eldon took his place. He propped a poster on the table. Dinner Dance Fundraiser! the poster proclaimed.

"Kate's has agreed to donate all the food if we do the serving and cleanup," Eldon said. "And Mountain Rose, a band over in Junction, will play for dancing afterwards. We're going to charge seventy-five dollars a person or a hundred dollars a couple."

"We're also going to have a silent auction to raise more money," Sheri added. She joined Eldon at the front of the room. "Every one of us will have to pitch in to make this happen, but we think it, along with the donor appeal, will be enough to meet our goal."

"Where are we going to hold this dinner and dance?" Ted asked.

"Right here." Sheri spread her arms wide to take in the big, concrete-floored space. "We'll need a decorating committee. We'll set up tables and chairs and a bar area, and leave space for a dance floor. We're working on getting businesses to donate everything else."

"You and Eldon and Ryan have done a terrific job," Carrie said. She led a round of applause. Sheri and Ryan grinned while Eldon flushed pink as everyone joined in with calls of "Thanks!" and "Way to go."

"Are we going to raise enough money to pay for a new Jaws?" Austen asked.

"One thing at a time," Carrie said. A search of all the equipment bays hadn't turned up the extractor, and everyone was certain it had not been in the Beast when the old Jeep burned.

"Do we have any idea what happened to it?" Eldon asked.

"None," Carrie said.

"Did you report the theft to the sheriff's department?" Sheri asked.

Carrie sighed. "I told them it was missing, but we don't know for certain that it was stolen."

"I did some checking, and nothing like that has come on the market," Jake said. "I looked around here, too. There was no sign of a break-in, and nothing else appears to have been taken."

The normally talkative crew fell silent, expressions reflecting various degrees of anger, frustration or discouragement as this latest revelation sank in.

"We can't worry about that now," Sheri said. She began laying out sheets of paper on the front table, next to the fundraising letter. "I've got sign-up lists here for decorating, waitstaff, predinner prep and after-party cleanup," she said. "I expect to see everyone's name on at least two sheets."

"And don't forget to sign the donor letter," Ryan added.

Carrie stepped up to be the first to sign. She chose prep work and cleanup. As temporary captain, she felt the need to be here for the entire event, and she definitely wanted to make sure the building was locked up tight afterward. She couldn't take a chance on any more equipment going missing.

She was signing the fundraising plea when Austen moved in beside her. "Where's Danny?" he asked.

"He texted to say he had to go out of town." She hadn't seen or spoken to Danny since they had rescued the family from the mudslide last week—and shared that scorching kiss. His silence troubled her, though she didn't like to admit how much. Obviously, he had been caught up in the emotion of the rescue and the kiss they shared hadn't meant anything.

At least, not to him.

"Where did he go?" Austen asked.

"He didn't say."

"Huh. I figured he would tell you."

"Well, he didn't." She regretted the sharp reply as soon as it was out of her mouth. "I'm sorry." She massaged her forehead. "It's been a long day." Her morning had begun with another tense phone call from Vance, who had an objection to almost every design decision she suggested for the Cornerstone project.

"You work so hard." Austen put a hand on her shoulder, then slid it over and began rubbing her back. "This hasn't been an easy time for you."

A shiver rippled down her spine at his touch and she stepped back, out of his reach, and handed him the pen she had been using. "I need to talk to Sheri," she said, and hurried away.

She joined Sheri and Eldon at the back of the room. "You two have done a terrific job," she said. "Thank you again."

"We haven't raised any money yet," Eldon said.

"We will," Carrie said. "I'm sure of it."

"Is everything okay?" Sheri peered closely at Carrie. "You look upset about something."

She was upset—about her job, about Danny avoiding her, about the loss of the Jaws and the theft of the money, about Austen getting too familiar. She shook her head. "I'm just tired."

"I'll try to hustle people along," Sheri said. "We could all use an early night."

"These accidents and stuff going missing has us all a little freaked-out," Eldon said as Sheri moved away. "I mean, everything points to one of the volunteers being behind it all, but I can't make myself believe it."

Carrie nodded. "I know." She scanned the gathering, lingering on each familiar face. Every one of them had a very personal reason for being part of this group. She couldn't believe anyone would want to destroy it.

"All right, people." Sheri spoke from the front of the room. "If I don't see your name on these lists, I *will* come find you."

Half an hour later, lists completed, chairs rearranged and lights out, Carrie locked the door and said good-night to Sheri and Eldon. Everyone else had left ahead of them. A few more minutes and she would be home. Maybe after she tucked in the kids, she would run a bubble bath and pour a glass of wine…

Her text alert sounded as she slid into the driver's seat of her SUV. Before she could read the message, her telephone rang.

"This is emergency dispatch," a pleasant woman's voice—Carrie recognized Darcie Davis—said. "We have a report of a vehicle off the road on Dakota Ridge, near Mile Marker 32."

Sheri and Eldon stood outside Carrie's car as she spoke to dispatch. She ended the call and lowered her window. "We got the page," Sheri said.

"We'd better unlock and go back inside," Carrie said. "The others will be here soon."

"Did dispatch have any details about what we might find at the accident site?" Sheri asked. "The text just said a car went off Dakota Ridge at Mile Marker 32."

"A motorist saw the skid marks and broken trees and called it in," Carrie said. She turned the key in the lock and shoved open the door. "They thought it must have just happened when they went by. No clue what kind of vehicle or how many people are involved."

"If I remember correctly, there's a drop-off there, but it's more gradual," Sheri said. "Still, we'll probably need climbing gear." She headed toward the area where the ropes were kept.

"I wish we had the Jaws," Eldon said. "It might come in handy if someone is trapped."

Carrie's phone rang and the screen showed a call from Ted. "Hello, Ted," she answered.

"I'm less than a mile from the accident site," he said. "I'll meet you there."

"There should be at least one deputy on-site," Carrie said.

Hannah and Jake were the next to arrive. She began assembling a medical kit, while Jake fetched a litter and helped Eldon load it into his truck. Ryan showed up and worked with Sheri on gathering the climbing gear. Austen and Carrie collected other items they might need, from signal flares to cervical collars and extra helmets. Everyone was calm and worked together smoothly. Less than twenty minutes from the initial text alerting them to the accident, they were headed toward the scene in three vehicles.

The red-and-blue strobe of the lights atop a Rayford County Sheriff's Department SUV guided them to the site, and they parked in a turnout just past it. Deputy Dwight Prentice met them in the road. "You can see where the vehicle slid off here," he said, and directed the beam of a flashlight over deep tire ruts in the soft shoulder of the road, then onto the broken brush at the lip of the drop-off. "I tried to look down there, but it's pitch-black and I couldn't see a thing."

"I'll get the portable spotlights," Jake said.

"I'll help," Austen said, and the two headed back to Jake's truck.

"Where's Ted?" Carrie asked the deputy.

She looked past him to Ted's truck, parked on the shoulder, just beyond the deputy's SUV.

"He said he was going to assess the situation." Dwight looked around. "I don't know where he went."

"I see a light down there." Hannah pointed into the drop-off. A beam, like a moving flashlight or headlamp, bobbed in the darkness.

Carrie cupped her hands to her mouth. "Ted!"

No answer. The light kept moving, away from them.

Carrie keyed her radio. "Ted, can you hear me?"

"I'm at the car." His voice came over the radio, a little breathless. "Looks like a Mini Cooper. On its side, roof of the vehicle pointed downhill. It's caught up in some brush. The driver is still inside. A young woman. I'm going to see if I can get closer."

"Ted, no!" Carrie's voice rose, so that the others

turned to stare. "Let a team get down to stabilize the vehicle first."

No answer. "Ted. Answer me!"

He didn't reply. Carrie turned to see Jake and Austen carrying two pole-mounted work lights, the kind used by highway crews for night work. They set them up and in a few minutes the area just below was flooded in white light.

The car was at the very edge of the light's reach, lying on its side like an injured animal. Carrie didn't see Ted at first, then she spotted him, beside the car. She keyed the radio again. "Ted, back off and wait," she said. "That's an order."

The radio crackled and his voice cut through the static. "There's just the driver. She's caught up in her seat belt, bleeding from a head wound, unconscious."

"We'll have people down in a minute to stabilize the vehicle." To her left, she could see Sheri and Eldon gathering equipment, preparing to scramble down.

"Ted?"

But he either didn't hear or was refusing to acknowledge. Carrie walked over to where Jake and Austen had joined the others. "I'm going to set an anchor and uncoil some rope on the descent that we can use going up and down," Sheri said.

"I've got cable and anchors for the car," Ryan said, already looping the coiled cable over head and shoulder. "Lucky it's a Mini Cooper. It won't take much to hold it."

"If it was anything heavier, it might already have slid on down," Eldon said.

Carrie stared down the slope once more. She couldn't see Ted. What was he doing down there?

"Tell Ted we're on our way," Sheri said. She tugged at the rope, which she had tied to an anchor driven into the ground, then started moving down the slope. "It's going to take a few minutes. There's a lot of loose rock."

"Take your time," Carrie said. "Ted?" She tried the mic again, but her only answer was static.

A terrible screech cut through the night air. Austen swore. Everyone froze and stared as the Mini Cooper slid across the rock, tumbled onto its roof, then disappeared into the darkness.

"Ted!" Carrie screamed the word. It took everything in her not to start running down the slope.

The radio crackled. "It's okay." Ted's voice sounded harsh in the sudden stillness. Breathless. "I'm okay."

"What happened?" It was Jake who spoke. Carrie's heart hammered so hard in her chest she couldn't find her voice.

"It's okay," Ted said. "I pulled her out in time. She's going to be okay."

"I told you to wait," Carrie said. Anger helped her find her tongue again.

"I had to go in and get her out," he said. "I could see the car was going to go. I had to do it."

Carrie realized the rest of the team was waiting for her to tell them what to do. "Go," she said. "Hannah, you too. Eldon, take the litter. Take care of the driver."

"An ambulance is on the way," Dwight said.

Carrie nodded. She took three deep breaths, then

lifted the radio to her lips once more. "Ted, I want you up here with me. Now."

She cut him off before he could argue and turned her attention to the others.

The next half hour passed in a blur as the team stabilized the young female driver. She regained consciousness as they worked, and Hannah determined she showed no signs of a serious head injury and had no broken bones or internal injuries, though she would be transported to the hospital for a more in-depth assessment. Six people together brought the litter up to the road and loaded it into the ambulance.

As the vehicle drove away, Carrie pulled Hannah aside. "What Ted did—pulling her out of the car—did it cause any further injury?" she asked.

Hannah shook her head, her expression troubled. "It didn't," she said. "But it could have if there had been any spinal damage, or broken bones."

Carrie nodded and went in search of Ted.

She found him by his truck, sitting on the bumper, scraping mud off the soles of his boots with a stick. "Ted, you violated every established protocol for accident response," she said. "Protocols you helped establish."

He looked up, mouth in a stubborn pout. "I saved her life," he said. "You ought to be focused on that. That's what we're about here, not protocols."

"If she had had spinal injuries, you could just as easily killed or crippled her when you pulled her from that car," Carrie said. She couldn't keep the shaking out of her voice. "And the car probably would have been fine if you hadn't started climbing on it to get to her."

"I did what had to be done," he said.

"You disobeyed a direct order," she said.

He stared at her, slit-eyed, his face pale in the harsh white glow of her headlamp.

"We're a team," she said. "No one acts alone. You know that. I'm relieving you of your duties as of this moment."

He stood, and she was aware of how much taller than her he was. He topped her by at least a foot. "You have no right to do that," he said.

"I'm your captain. The team granted me that right."

"Tony is our captain."

"And Tony isn't here." She deliberately turned her back on him and saw the others, moving in a group toward them. "Go home, Ted," she said.

He saw the others, too. "I saved that girl's life," he said.

Ryan shook his head. "You'd better go home," he said, his voice gentle.

"Is that how you all feel?" he demanded. "You're taking her side."

"She's the captain," Sheri said. The others nodded.

Carrie bit the inside of her cheek, fighting tears—of exhaustion, and from a swell of pride and gratitude for their support. She didn't turn around, only listened as a truck door slammed, the engine roared to life, then Ted drove away, tires spitting gravel.

Sheri was the first to reach her. She put an arm

around Carrie's shoulders. "You did the right thing," she whispered.

Carrie nodded. She believed that, but her belief hadn't made the decision any easier. She took another deep breath and raised her head to face them. "Good job tonight," she said. "Now, let's go home and get some rest." She didn't believe she would get much sleep tonight. Days like this had a way of replaying themselves all night long. As if living through it once wasn't enough.

Chapter Thirteen

Danny had signed up to wait tables and help with cleanup at the dinner dance, and he arrived to find search and rescue headquarters transformed by a jungle of plants, fairy lights and white-clothed tables. "The dinner sold out!" Sheri informed him as she rushed by with a tray of candles, which she began distributing among the tables.

He followed her, lighting the candles and straightening chairs. All around the room, fellow volunteers hauled in ice, arranged the bandstand and bar areas, and bustled about. He scanned the room, searching for Carrie. He hadn't seen her since the kiss they had shared on the side of the road. She probably thought he was the biggest coward ever, running away from her like that. He hadn't been avoiding her, exactly, but he hadn't provided any details beyond "family stuff" after his sister had summoned him to deal with another setback involving their mother. After spending ten days out of town dealing with that situation, he had worked extra shifts at the surgery center to make up for the time he had missed and had continued to put off contacting Carrie. After all, maybe she didn't even want to see him. As long as he had known her, she had kept pretty much every man at arm's length, so why should he be different? Maybe it was smarter to keep quiet about his feelings for her than risk rejection.

"You sure clean up nice," a woman said from behind him. He turned and smiled at Hannah, who was looking very pretty herself in a short, sparkly dress with a full skirt, a far cry from her paramedic's uniform.

"You look great," he said, and hugged her. He was glad he and Hannah could be friends now, and that she was happy. Over his shoulder, he spotted Jake, who, like Danny, wore a dark suit and well-shined shoes.

"If you're looking for Carrie, she's out back, talking to the caterers," Hannah said.

"I, um, just wanted to explain why I haven't been around much lately," he said.

Hannah sent him a questioning look. "She knows you were dealing with family stuff, right? I'm sure she said that. I hope everything is okay?"

The question invited an explanation, but he had a policy of not talking about his family. It was better that way. "It's fine," he said. "And I understand you only had one callout while I was gone?"

"A girl in a Mini Cooper slid off Dakota Ridge," Hannah said. She leaned closer and lowered her voice. "You heard about Ted, right?"

"Ryan filled me in. What was Ted thinking? He and that girl could have both been killed. As long as he's been in search and rescue, he knows that."

Hannah shrugged. “He says he didn’t have a choice, but I don’t really believe it. Maybe he was trying to prove himself, you know? Anyway, none of us have seen or heard from him. I’m worried about him.”

“Maybe I’ll get a chance to go see him,” Danny said. “I wasn’t there, so maybe it won’t be as awkward as if someone else went.”

“That would be great if you did that,” she said. “Maybe you can find out what was going through his head.” She glanced to the side. “Here’s Carrie now. Talk to her. I know she feels bad about what happened.”

Anything Danny had been prepared to say fled from his mind at the sight of Carrie making her way toward him. Her dress was a solid royal blue, of some shimmery material that slid over her curves, and a V-neckline showed just a hint of cleavage. She had caught her blond hair up in a sparkly clip, with a few loose strands framing her face. “Danny!” Her smile was tentative. Hopeful.

“It’s great to see you,” he said. “You look amazing.”

Her smile brightened a few watts. “So do you!”

“I’m sorry I’ve been AWOL lately,” he said. “I want to explain.” He had no idea what he would say, but he owed it to her to try.

“Carrie! Where should we set up the table for the silent-auction donations?” someone asked from behind a cluster of potted palms on the other side of the room.

“I have to go,” she said, and turned and hurried away.

Then Eldon called him to help move some storage

totes to make room for another table, guests started arriving and the evening was off. Danny focused on greeting people, taking drink orders and serving the food, but all the while he was aware of Carrie, moving among the tables, talking to the guests. Why had he ever stayed away from her? He only hoped he would have a chance to get close to her again.

"THIS MAY BE the best fundraiser we ever had," Carrie told Sheri as they stood at the edge of the dance floor after dinner, watching couples sway to a sentimental ballad from the band.

"It's certainly the most fun," Sheri said. "We've raised $2,500 from ticket sales, and should bring in more from the silent auction. And our letter-writing campaign is starting to pull in donations, too. I'm feeling more confident about reaching our goal."

Austen joined them. Like the other male volunteers, he wore a suit and tie, his complete with a black-and-gold brocade vest, which gave him the look of an Old West gambler. "Great turnout, isn't it?" he asked.

"It is," Carrie agreed.

"And no trouble from whoever has been harassing us," he said.

"Don't even mention that person," Sheri said.

He turned to Carrie. "May I have this dance?"

Carrie looked around. Several of the other volunteers were dancing—she spotted Hannah and Jake across the room, and Ryan with his girlfriend, Deni Traynor.

"Go on," Sheri said. "Enjoy yourself."

She walked with Austen onto the dance floor and took his hand. "You look especially beautiful tonight," he said.

"It's always a shock to see our fellow volunteers so dressed up," she said. "For instance, I never would have guessed you were the type to own a fancy vest. It's gorgeous."

He smirked. "There's a lot you don't know about me."

She could say the same about all her fellow volunteers. There was so much she didn't know about Danny, for instance, including where he had disappeared to for the last two weeks. He said he wanted to tell her, but she was half-afraid to hear his explanation.

"Carrie? Did you hear what I said?"

She shifted her attention back to Austen. "I'm sorry. What was that?"

"I said, do you have any more ideas about who might be making all this trouble for search and rescue?"

She shook her head. "I don't want to talk about that tonight."

"Sorry. I didn't mean to upset you."

"Excuse me." At the sound of the familiar voice she looked over to see Danny beside them. He smiled at her and she caught her breath. Since when could a smile make her feel this way? "May I cut in?" he asked. Then, not waiting for an answer, he took her hand and she moved into his arms.

"Hey!" Austen protested, but Danny whisked her away.

"Was that very rude of me?" he asked.

"Maybe just a little." She resisted the urge to look back at Austen. She wanted to keep her focus on Danny, on the feel of his arm at her back and his fingers entwined in hers.

"You looked like you might welcome an interruption," he said. "You were frowning."

"Was I? Austen wanted to talk about whoever is behind all the attacks on SAR. I told him I didn't want to think about that tonight."

"No," Danny said. "Not now. It's a night for celebrating."

"Celebrating all the money we're raising?" she asked.

"I was thinking about celebrating that we're still a tight team. It's taken every one of us to pull this off."

"That's a good thing to celebrate," she said. "And you're right. Everyone is working so hard."

"Especially you. We might have fallen apart after Tony was hurt, but you kept us all together."

She ought to have been elated by this compliment, but regret dulled her happiness. "Ted should be here," she said. "This organization always meant so much to him."

"I heard what happened," Danny said. "You did the right thing."

"I did." She sighed. "But I hate it turned out this way. I know he's been fretting over his diminishing role with the team, but that wasn't the way to assert himself."

"I'm thinking of going to see him next week," Danny said. "Maybe I can get him to talk to me."

"That would be wonderful." She squeezed his hand. "Thank you." She glanced around them once more, as much to keep from staring at him as anything. Being here in his arms felt so intimate, yet she was conscious of everyone around them. "A night like tonight reminds me of how much support we really do get from the community," she said.

"I think most people realize any one of them might need us at any time." He grinned. "We could put that on a T-shirt—Search and Rescue, Not Just for Clueless Tourists."

She laughed, and felt the knot she had been carrying around in her stomach loosen a little. Maybe this wasn't the serious conversation she and Danny needed to have, but it was a step in the right direction.

THE DANCING LASTED until midnight, when the music stopped and Carrie and Sheri thanked the remaining guests for attending and announced the silent-auction winners. Then the cleanup work began. Almost everyone pitched in to help, including volunteers who hadn't signed up for the duty. Within half an hour they had the tables put away, the decorations taken down and the plants arranged by the door, ready to go back to the florist who had loaned them out for the evening.

Danny stayed near Carrie as much as possible, and lingered until they were the only two left.

"Leave the plants and I'll get them back tomorrow," Carrie said.

"I can help with that," he said.

"You don't have to," she said. "I know you're busy."

"I was busy, but I'm not now." He took her hand. "That's one of the things I wanted to talk to you about."

"You don't owe me any explanations," she protested, though she didn't pull away.

"I think I do." He led her to the old sofa, which had been moved back to its usual spot at the side of the room. "Just let me say this, okay?"

"Of course."

They sat, and he let go of her hand, aware that he hadn't prepared for this moment. "So, you know I left town to deal with some family stuff."

"That's what your text said, yes."

"It was true. I know I was vague, but it's not something I really talk about."

"You don't have to tell me—"

"I want to tell you." He wanted her to know this about him, something he didn't share with anyone else. "I went to see my mom, in Iowa. She has... well, she has mental health issues. Several different diagnoses, none of them pleasant or easy. She's fine when she takes her medication. That is, she's able to function pretty well. My sister is there and she helps look after Mom, but sometimes, Mom decides to stop taking the medication and bad things can happen." He paused, reflecting on all the ways that had played out over the years. No need to go into that. "Joy—my sister—can't handle Mom when it gets really bad, so she calls me. I'm usually able to talk her into getting treatment, going back on her meds."

"Oh, Danny. How awful for all of you."

The sympathy in her voice and her expression

made his throat tighten. "It can be pretty awful, but we're used to it. It's just what we have to do." He had spent a lot of time when he was younger being angry that he didn't have a mother who did the things his friend's mothers did, or the kind of relationship children ought to have with a parent. Now he accepted this was the way things were. He told himself he didn't need anyone to lean on. He did fine on his own and always had. Most of the time he even believed it.

"Is she okay now?" Carrie asked.

"As okay as she ever gets." He met her eyes, letting her see that he was calm. He was fine. "She was in an inpatient treatment center for a week. She's home now and Joy says she's doing okay. She's upset with me for putting her in the hospital, so she isn't talking to me right now, but she'll get over it."

"I'm sorry." She took his hand and squeezed it and he had to fight not to pull her close.

"After I got home, I needed to make up a lot of shifts at the surgery center," he said. "And I didn't really feel like talking to anyone."

"I can understand that."

"But I wanted to talk to you," he said. He took a deep breath, the way he did before starting a steep descent into a canyon, or anything else that scared him. "That kiss we shared—that was really special. To me, at least. I thought about it a lot while I was gone. I thought about it when things got hard."

"It was special to me, too." She leaned in and touched his cheek, then stretched up and brought her lips to his.

He froze, afraid to move as her mouth pressed to his, afraid of the storm of emotion that threatened to overwhelm them both. This is what he had thought of when his mother was raging at him or weeping or flailing at him with her fists as he tried to keep her from hurting herself—of being here with Carrie. Of holding her and her holding him.

She wrapped her arms around him, and her warmth melted his last resistance. He groaned and returned the kiss. He had so much he wanted to say to her, but he couldn't find the words. So he tried to let the kiss convey his emotions, all the pent-up longing and tender feelings conveyed through the press of his lips and caress of his hands. He slid his hands down her sides, shaping his fingers to her firm curves, pressing his body against hers, letting her feel how much he wanted her.

She pulled him down on top of her, one leg wrapped around his thigh, her tongue teasing the sensitive nerves of his inner lip. It took everything in him to pull away—just for a second. "Do you want to go back to my place?" he asked, his voice ragged.

She smiled up at him, a wicked, sexy look that had his heart racing even faster. "We could—or we could stay here," she said.

"Good idea." The sofa was comfortable enough, and the dim light lent an intimacy to the setting. And really, what did it matter where they were? He didn't intend for either of them to focus on their surroundings. "Give me a second," he said.

He made himself get up and move to one of the bins where they kept the medical kits. He fished out a foil-wrapped condom and returned to the sofa.

Carrie laughed. "I wondered if anyone ever used those," she said.

He eyed the gold packet. "I never have," he said. "But the wilderness-medicine course I took emphasized that you could use them to protect digits or as a makeshift tourniquet, so we keep a few on hand."

Smiling, she took the packet from him. "Why don't you make sure the door is locked? We don't want to be disturbed."

While Danny crossed the room to check the door, Carrie slipped off her dress and undergarments. The look on Danny's face when he returned to the sofa and found her naked was worth her slight self-consciousness. Danny wasted no time undressing, and she was happy to lie back and admire his muscular shoulders and legs and firm abs. All that training for rescue work had some definite physical benefits.

He retrieved a couple of blankets from the supply closet and joined her on the sofa once more. "This is nice, isn't it?" he said as he snuggled against her, then bent to kiss her again.

It had been a long time for her, but she was pretty sure sex was never this good before. Danny lived up to his reputation as a skilled lover, considerate and tender, making sure she enjoyed herself while clearly also enjoying himself. He took his time, touching and admiring her and encouraging her to do the same.

Just the feel of him beneath her hands was exciting, and the easy way he laughed off the awkwardness of trying to arrange themselves on the narrow sofa was its own kind of foreplay.

By the time he knelt over her, condom in place, she was trembling with eagerness. She caressed his hips and lifted her own to guide him inside. She closed her eyes and let out a low moan as he filled her, the sensation almost overwhelming, but so, so good.

She felt the tension of him holding back, and urged him to move faster and go deeper, but he insisted on slowing things down, building the moment until, when her climax finally overtook her, she cried out and gripped him hard. When she opened her eyes, he was smiling down at her, and her emotions overwhelmed her so much she had to bite her lip to keep from telling him she loved him. She was sure such a declaration would send him running away. And really, what she loved was the way he made her feel right now, and that was something different, wasn't it?

Afterward, they lay in each other's arms with the blankets draped over them. She snuggled against him, and fought the desire to stay here all night, his arms wrapped around her, his warmth seeping into her. Instead, she forced herself to raise her head from his shoulder and brush the hair out of her eyes. "I wish I could stay, but I need to get home," she said. That was one reason she hadn't wanted to go back to his place. Leaving his bed would have been even harder than getting up off this sofa.

He nodded and sat up. "I meant what I said earlier—I'll help you with those plants tomorrow."

"If you really want to do that." She wasn't going to say no to help—or to seeing him again.

"I really want to see you again," he said as if he had read her thoughts.

"All right. But not too early."

"After lunch? I'll try to visit Ted in the morning and I can report back to you."

She kissed him again. A quick press of her mouth to his, then pulling away before she was tempted to linger. "Thank you."

"I'm the one who should be thanking you. I was sure my disappearing act had ruined my chances with you. I just… I tend to be cautious about relationships."

"Me too." So many emotions weighted those two words. She wanted to ask him where he thought things would go between them after tonight. But she didn't dare. She wasn't prepared to hear that he wasn't ready for a commitment, that a woman with two children was too much, that he was happy to be with her as long as she didn't take things too seriously.

Right. She could try that, couldn't she? Her heart ached at the thought, and she leaned over and picked up her dress from the floor. "I'll see you tomorrow," she said.

They dressed in silence, then put the blankets in the bin to be washed and fluffed up the cushions on the sofa. Danny walked her to her car and gave her the kind of kiss that made her think he wanted her to spend the next few hours thinking about him. No doubt she would do that, but she would try to focus on reliving what had been. She wouldn't let herself anticipate the future. She wouldn't allow herself to hope too much.

Chapter Fourteen

Danny woke far too early, wishing Carrie were there with him. Once she had decided to take a chance on him, she hadn't held back, and he loved that about her. He might even be falling in love with her—scary thought. He immediately pushed away the idea. No sense complicating a good thing with something as unreliable as love.

He rose and dressed and after coffee and a bagel, he got into his truck, made a brief stop in town, then headed out County Road 7 to the Lazy S Ranch. As far as he could tell, Ted didn't do a lot of actual ranching these days. He leased part of the property to a younger man who grazed cattle there some of the year.

Ted's truck was parked in front of the house, a long, low cedar-sided structure in need of paint. Ted opened the door when Danny was halfway up the walk. "What are you doing here?" he asked.

"I wanted to hear your side of what happened with search and rescue," Danny said.

Ted stepped aside and held the door open wider. He looked the same—freshly shaved, dressed in jeans and a button-up Western shirt. He didn't look like a man who was losing it.

"I brought donuts," Danny said, and held up the bag.

Ted took the sack. "I've got coffee in the kitchen." He led the way through a darkened living room to a kitchen with faded, yellow-striped wallpaper and a metal kitchen table with mismatched chairs. He filled two white ceramic mugs with coffee—black—and sat at the table. "What did they tell you happened?" he asked.

"You were first on the scene and didn't wait for the others," Danny said. He took a donut and bit into it.

"Yeah, well, the car wasn't in a good position." He sipped his coffee. "I think it would have slid on down if I hadn't grabbed the girl when I did."

"What would you tell a rookie who did something like that?" Danny asked.

"I'm not a rookie."

Danny said nothing, but he didn't look away, either.

Ted shifted in his chair. "I've been with search and rescue longer than anybody else," he said. "That ought to earn me the benefit of the doubt."

"When I joined the group, you told me search and rescue isn't about individual heroes. It's about the team."

Ted stared down at the table. Danny was surprised to see that his scalp showed through his hair in places at the top of his head. "Carrie kicked me out," he said.

"She hasn't committed anything to record," Danny said. "There's been no formal report."

"Everybody knows what happened."

"Everybody still thinks of you as the founding member who stayed with the group the longest. You could keep that reputation."

"What am I supposed to do—just resign?"

"Isn't that better than being kicked out?"

The silence stretched so thin Danny could hear the warmer on the coffee machine cycling on and off. He finished the donut and sipped the last of the coffee. "Somebody will need to take the old climbing ropes to Luray Elgin," Ted said finally, "if I'm not going to be around to see to it."

"Is she the woman who makes rugs out of climbing rope?" Danny asked.

"Yeah. You ever seen them?"

Danny shook his head.

"They're pretty amazing looking—all those bright colors. We give her the retired ropes that aren't safe for climbing and she donates 20 percent of her profits to Eagle Mountain Search and Rescue."

"I'll make sure she gets the ropes," Danny said.

Ted nodded and picked out a donut. "What do you think you'll do with all your free time?" Danny asked.

"I've been thinking of writing a book."

Danny tried to hide his surprise but was pretty sure he failed. "A book?"

"Yeah." Ted grinned. "I'm not an ignorant cowboy, you know. I read a lot. I'm thinking of writing a history of Eagle Mountain Search and Rescue."

"You're the perfect person to do that," Danny said.

"I am."

They made small talk after that, about the fund-raising dance, Ted's ranch and stories he might put in his book. Before Danny knew it, it was almost noon. He slid back his chair. "I'd better go. I promised Carrie I'd help her return some plants we borrowed for the dinner dance."

"How did that go?" Ted asked.

"It went well. I think we raised several thousand dollars, and Sheri says more donations are coming in all the time."

"That's good." Ted shoved to his feet. "Tell Carrie I'll turn in my letter of resignation in a few days. She can throw a party."

"You deserve a party," Danny said. Yes, the older man had made a mistake, but that didn't take away from all he had done before.

Carrie was waiting out front when Danny arrived at SAR headquarters. She moved into his arms and kissed him eagerly. He wondered what she would think if he suggested another session on the sofa. She must have been thinking the same thing, because she stepped back. "I only have an hour before I need to get back home," she said.

"Then, we'd better get the plants loaded."

It only took a few minutes to arrange all the pots in the back of Carrie's SUV. "Did you see Ted this morning?" she asked when they were done.

"Yes. And he's calmed down a lot." He shared the gist of their conversation, including the information about Luray Elgin and Ted's message that he would be resigning.

"We'll throw him a farewell bash," Carrie said. "And I'll make sure the newspaper knows all he's done for the organization over the years."

"He'll like that. And you're bound to still hear from him regularly. He seems serious about writing a history of SAR."

"That would be wonderful."

Danny checked his watch. "There's just one more thing. I want to take a look and see how much rope Ted has set aside for Luray," he said. "He keeps it all in the boiler room, so it doesn't get mixed up with the good rope."

"Sure. Let's take a look." She led the way to the back of the building, and a door marked Boiler. He opened it, then reached up and pulled the chain on the overhead light to illuminate a space that contained the dark metal boiler, a mop bucket and some gallon jugs of cleaners, and a large wooden crate overflowing with a tangle of multicolored climbing rope.

"Looks like it's been a while since Ted made a delivery to Luray," Danny said. He bent and tried to heft the crate, but it wouldn't budge.

"All that rope is bound to be heavy," Carrie said.

"It is." He straightened and frowned at the tangle "But not that heavy." He grasped a coil and tugged it out of the way. "Help me get some of this out of here," he said.

She helped him pull at the lines until a mass of them came free and tumbled onto the floor of the boiler room. He spotted a glimpse of orange beneath the rope.

"What is that?" Carrie asked, and reached in to clear more rope.

But Danny was faster. He leaned past her and pulled at the object at the bottom of the crate. He lifted the hydraulic extractor—the Jaws of Life—onto the pile of cords between them.

Carrie stared. "Did Ted put that there?" she asked.

"I don't know," Danny said. "But we need to find out."

TED GREETED THEM at the door to his house, coffee mug in hand. He slid his gaze over Carrie, then addressed Danny. "What are you two doing here?"

"We need to talk." Carrie said. "Please?"

"I already told Danny I'm sorry about what happened," Ted said. "I don't need you to lecture me about what I did wrong."

"No lectures," she promised. She wasn't angry with Ted, at least not anymore. Going after that girl on his own had been wrong, but no one had been hurt and she believed he regretted his actions. But hiding the Jaws from the rest of them was another story. She needed to understand why he would have done such a thing.

"We found the Jaws," Danny said. "The extractor."

"That's good," Ted said. "Where was it?"

"Can we come in?" Danny asked.

Ted turned and led them through a room that reminded Carrie of her uncle's place before he remarried—worn furniture, dust on the tables beneath a clutter of old magazines and books, and half-empty coffee mugs and glasses. A room that was a little neglected, just like the man himself.

On the wall by the door to the kitchen were a series of plaques—awards Ted had received over his years with search and rescue. Volunteer of the Year. For service as search and rescue captain. A state award for outstanding service. The plaques were dusted. Shiny. Loved.

"Coffee?" he asked, already filling his mug from an old-fashioned coffee machine beside the sink.

"No thanks," Carrie said.

"Nothing for me," Danny said. He lowered himself into a chair on one side of the vintage metal and Formica table. Carrie sat across from him and Ted took the chair at the end.

"You two look like you're getting ready to face a firing squad," Ted said. "Or maybe you're the ones who are going to do the shooting." He sipped his coffee. "What's this about?"

"We found the Jaws of Life," Danny said.

"Yeah, you said that. Where was it?"

"It was under the discarded climbing ropes in the storage closet," Carrie said.

"Huh." He set the coffee mug down with a thump! "Who put it there?"

Carrie looked to Danny. What had seemed so obvious when they had been standing in that closet together wasn't so clear now. Was Ted really this good of an actor?

"We thought maybe you did," Danny said.

Ted's shoulders slumped. "You think I'd put some

poor person's life in danger with a stupid prank like that?" There was more hurt than anger in the words.

Carrie reached out and touched his hand. "I don't know what to think, Ted," she said. Not now, after seeing him here like this, and remembering all search and rescue had meant to him. "Do you know anything that could help us?"

He shook his head, and lifted the coffee mug to his lips once more. The fingers that wrapped around the handle of the mug were creased and scarred—hands that had gripped ropes and carried litters and cradled injured people in canyons and on mountain-tops where most people wouldn't go.

"When was the last time you were in that storage closet?" Danny asked.

"I don't know," Ted said.

"Think," Danny said. "The Jaws went missing three weeks ago. Was it before or after that?"

Ted set the mug down again. "It was before that. After Tony fell, when we checked all the ropes. Sheri and Ryan and I went through the lot and pulled out a couple that were near their expiration date. I took them in there and added them to the pile. I remember thinking I needed to take them to Luray, but then it slipped my mind. I haven't been in there since."

"Have you seen anyone else in there?" Carrie asked.

"It's just a closet," he said, an edge to his voice. "Anybody could go in there. Somebody who needed cleaning supplies, for instance."

"The extractor was hidden under the coils of rope,"

Danny said. "Someone just looking in there wouldn't have seen it. We didn't see it until we picked up the rope."

"Well, I didn't put it there. But I sure don't belong with search and rescue anymore if you think I would."

His lips trembled and Carrie looked away. "I know you wouldn't do anything to hurt anyone," she said. "You've been the anchor of our organization for years and I'm going to make sure people don't forget that." She stood, and Danny rose also, but Ted stayed seated.

"I'm not the one behind all these things happening to SAR," Ted said. "But I hope you find the person who is. So far they've managed not to hurt anyone badly, but pretty soon our luck is going to run out. Someone is going to end up dead, whether it's someone from SAR, or a person we could have saved."

She nodded. It had been easy to dismiss most of their persecutor's actions as petty, but Tony had almost died from his accident, and hiding the Extractor could have had really serious consequences if they needed the equipment to get someone in distress out of a vehicle. "We're doing everything we can," she said, but even as she said the words, she knew that wasn't enough.

She waited until they were back in Danny's car before she spoke. "We can't just wait for the next bad thing to happen," she said. "We need to do more to find the person behind all these incidents."

"What else can we do?" he asked.

"I was hoping you had an idea."

"I have lots of ideas, but nothing to do with that."

She turned to him and he winked, which made her laugh in spite of everything. He took her hand. "Maybe if we put our heads together, and list everything we know about these incidents, we'll see some common thread," he said. "We'll notice some person who was involved every time."

"That's a good idea. But I have to be home." She glanced at her watch. "In five minutes. My mom is going out with friends and I can't leave my kids alone."

"Why don't I take these ropes to Luray and bring dinner over in a few hours? After we eat, we can make a list."

She hesitated. Inviting him over was a big step—something that signaled he was more than just a fellow volunteer. Still, her kids knew and liked him.

"Is that not a good idea?" he asked.

"No. It's a great idea." She smiled, and hoped she was successful at hiding her doubts. "The kids will love it. And so will I."

It's just a casual dinner, she reminded herself. It didn't have to mean anything.

INCIDENT #1: TONY'S FALL

People present: Carrie, Danny, Ted, Sheri, Ryan, Eldon, Hannah, Austen, Tony

Incident #2: Beast burned

People present: ???

Incident #3: Austen run off road

People present: Everyone was at the meeting. (Austen and Ted were both late)

Incident #4: Money stolen from fair

People present: Austen, Sheri (other volunteers were at the fair)

Incident #5: Jaws goes missing

People present: Everyone except Hannah

Incident #6: Carrie's tires flattened

People present: Everyone except Sheri, Hannah, and Ted.

Heads together, Carrie and Danny studied the chart they had made. Their take-out dinner of Chinese food had been cleared away, though the scent of cashew chicken and shrimp lo mein lingered. Dylan and Amber were in the other room, playing a noisy game of checkers, which Amber had only recently learned to do and was determined to never lose. The children had been comically blasé about Danny's arrival with dinner, though Carrie had caught them sending excited looks to one another. Whether because she had invited a man home or because she had invited this particular man, she couldn't be sure. She had chosen to ignore them, and Danny either hadn't noticed or was playing it cool also.

"Almost all the rescuers were at or near the scene at the time of most of the incidents," Carrie said. "Jake and Hannah and you were away for part of the time—but I never suspected you—or Sheri, Jake or Hannah, for that matter."

"That's the problem—we don't want to suspect anyone." Danny leaned back in his chair. "Ted still had the most opportunity, to my mind. And you have to admit, he hasn't been acting himself lately."

"I can't believe it," she said. She looked at the chart again. "I can't believe any of it, really."

"Maybe we should talk to Jake," Danny said. "Find out if the Sheriff's department has come up with anything they're not telling us. And we should tell them about finding the Jaws."

"You're right. I'll call tomorrow and set up a meeting." She stifled a yawn.

Danny slid back his chair. "I'd better go. Thanks for dinner."

"You bought the dinner," she said. He had refused to let her reimburse him.

"Then, thanks for your company." He kissed her cheek. "Your kids are great, by the way."

"They are." She walked him to the door, aware of a sudden silence in the other room. Danny shrugged into his jacket, gave her another kiss on the cheek and left. She waited until he was in his car, then turned toward the living room. Dylan and Amber both stared intently at the checkerboard. "Cut the act, you two," she said. "I know you were spying on us."

Dylan wrinkled his nose. "That wasn't much of a kiss good-night."

"What do you know about it?" Amber asked. She looked up at her mother. "I like him," she said, with such a sweet smile it made a lump in Carrie's throat.

Carrie held out her arms. "Come here, you two."

They came and let her hug them close—something

Dylan was less and less inclined to allow. "Is Danny your boyfriend?" Amber asked.

Was he? "Maybe," Carrie said. "But whatever he is, the two of you still come first. Understand?"

They both nodded, solemn, and allowed one last hug before Dylan squirmed away. "Tell him he can bring over Chinese food anytime," he said.

The front door opened. "I'm home," Becky called. A few moments later, she came into the living room.

"How was your evening?" Carrie asked.

"It was good. You know Clara and Marie and I always have a good time. How was yours?"

"Danny came over and brought us Chinese," Amber volunteered.

"Oh, he did?" Becky sent her daughter a look full of questions. "Search and rescue business?"

"He kissed her good-night," Dylan said, then collapsed into giggles.

Carrie cursed her tendency to blush so easily. "I think it's time for a certain boy and girl to go to bed," she said.

She spent the next half hour getting her children off to sleep. Her mother was waiting in the kitchen when Carrie returned. Becky was studying the chart they had made. "Is this everything that has happened with SAR?" Becky asked.

"Yes. Danny and I were trying to see if there was any commonality among all the incidents that we had missed."

"It's good to have another adult to bounce ideas off of," Becky said.

Carrie sensed a question mark at the end of this statement, an invitation for her to say more about her relationship with Danny Irwin. "We're just…getting to know each other," she said. "It's early days. Don't read too much into it."

"I won't," Becky said. "But it's good to see you happy."

Was she happy? Sometimes, she was ecstatic. Also confused. And afraid. Nervous about messing this up. Hoping for more than was probably possible.

In other words, everything was proceeding in a perfectly normal way. The way life always seemed to do.

Chapter Fifteen

Monday morning, Danny was coming out of the coffee shop when he spotted Deputy Jake Gwynn across the street. Jake waved and Danny crossed over to fall into step beside the deputy. “Did Carrie call you?” Danny asked.

“She did. She told me the two of you found the hydraulic extractor in the supply closet.”

“Yes, and we can’t figure out who put it there. Has the investigation turned up anything?”

Jake shook his head. “No. These events are so random and seemingly unconnected, and so far whoever is responsible isn’t leaving behind any evidence. I’m sorry I don’t have better news for you.”

“Do you still think a volunteer is behind all the harassment?” Danny asked.

“I don’t see how someone from outside the organization could have committed those crimes,” Jake said. “At least, the attempt on Tony’s life and the arson to the Beast were crimes. A good defense attorney would probably argue that the extractor was just misplaced.”

"It wasn't misplaced," Danny said.

"I know. I'm just saying what would probably happen in court," Jake said. "It's not enough to be suspicious about someone. We have to have a lot of proof in order to make an arrest."

Danny sipped his coffee, wishing he had some kind of proof to offer, but there was nothing.

"Whoever it is hasn't done anything recently," Jake said. "Maybe they're tired of it. Or something happened to scare them off."

"It doesn't feel good knowing someone I have to depend on in a bind could be behind this," Danny said. "And that they've gotten away with it. Tony could have died. That's attempted murder."

"If we find the person responsible, we'll charge them, but right now we just don't have evidence."

They reached the public lot where Danny had parked his car. "I have to get to work," he said. "It was good talking to you, even if the news wasn't what I wanted to hear."

"We'll let you know if we turn up anything new," Jake said. "We're not going to give up."

Danny's mood didn't improve as he drove to work. He couldn't shake the feeling that he was letting Carrie down. This was what he hated about getting too close to other people—this feeling that he wasn't doing enough to help. He had spent his whole life feeling that way with his mom and though he knew it was wrong, he could never completely lose the guilt.

He was in the employee locker room, about to begin his shift, when his supervisor, Helene, leaned around the doorway. "Danny, can I see you in my office a minute?" she asked.

He doubted anyone heard those words and didn't feel a clench in their stomach. He shut the door to his locker. "Sure," he said, and followed her to the cramped space that served as her office. Helene, a cheerful, round-faced woman with a mass of short blond curls, settled into the worn desk chair.

"Don't look so worried," she said as he sat in the chair across from her, his knees pressed against the metal front of her desk. "This is good news."

"What is it?" he asked, still wary.

"A supervisory position has come open and I want to recommend you."

"What supervisory position?" Usually, the rumor mill broadcast this kind of thing for weeks before any official announcement.

"Actually, I'm leaving to take a position with the hospital in Junction." She smiled. "I want you to take over here."

Both of these statements—that she was leaving and that she wanted him to replace her—surprised him. "You know I'm not interested in supervising anyone," he said.

"That's what you always say, but Danny, you've got more experience than everybody else. And you're good with people—patients and coworkers. You could do this. It would mean more pay, a step up the ladder."

He shook his head. "I'm not interested."

"At least think about it." She smiled in a way he

thought was meant to be encouraging. "You're not getting any younger."

"You're not getting any younger" was code for "Isn't it about time you grew up?" Stepped up. Took responsibility. But all being responsible had brought him was more disappointment. Why take the risk when he didn't have to?

CARRIE'S PHONE CONVERSATION with Jake Monday morning left her frustrated. If the sheriff's department, with their access to forensic testing and computer databases couldn't come up with anything that even pointed to a suspect in all the crimes that had been committed against search and rescue, what chance did the rest of them have of stopping whoever was responsible before someone was seriously hurt?

This was still on her mind when she sat at her desk later that morning. A large yellow sticky note on her computer screen said "See me about the Cornerstone project!" in bold letters printed with a marker. The note wasn't signed, but she didn't have to wonder who it was from. Bracing herself for the worst, she rose and went to Greg Abernathy's office.

"You wanted to see me?" she asked.

Abernathy looked up from his monitor. As usual, he was dressed straight out of a Ralph Lauren ad, his leather vest too uncreased and his boots too unscuffed to pass for authentic. "Miles Lindberg isn't happy with the plans for his new building," he said.

She waited, refraining from pointing out that those plans weren't the ones she had originally drawn up for Lindberg. The ones he had been enthusiastic about when she had shown him the preliminaries.

"You need to redo them," he said.

"What, exactly, does he want changed?"

"He wants a walled courtyard connecting the new and old construction."

"That was in my original drawings." She should have stopped there but couldn't help herself. "The ones Vance changed."

"No, it wasn't," he snapped. "You don't know what you're talking about."

She drew in a long, slow breath. "I'll call Mike and find out exactly what he wants," she said.

"No!" Abernathy rose, both hands flat on the desk, leaning toward her. "I'll have Vance do it. You don't need to talk to Mike."

"Part of getting the plans right is consulting with the client," she said. "I need his input to do a good job."

"Vance will tell you what to do," Abernathy said. "This is his project now. You're his assistant."

It was my project until you gave it away, she thought. Her stomach hurt, and the tension at the back of her neck foretold an imminent headache—one that probably wouldn't go away as long as Abernathy and Vance were in this office.

Or as long as she was.

The truth of that thought came into her head with blinding clarity. Yes, this was the only architectural firm in Eagle Mountain. The only employer who would give her the flexibility she needed to be with her children. But what was stopping her from changing that?

There was no law saying she couldn't open her own firm, and make her own rules. She held her breath, letting the idea sink in. It was ridiculous. Foolish. She had a family to support. A reputation to protect.

Abernathy wasn't doing her reputation any favors, though. Not as long as he refused to give her more responsibility and blamed her for other people's mistakes. She met his gaze directly. "You'll have my letter of resignation within the hour," she said, surprised at how calm she sounded.

"What?" The word emerged as the squawk of a startled rooster. "You can't resign."

"I can, and I will." Not waiting for more, she turned and retreated, not to her desk, but to the ladies' room, the one place she could be sure Abernathy wouldn't follow. Once sure she was alone, she pulled out her telephone and called her mother.

"Carrie? Is everything all right?" Becky sounded alarmed—probably because Carrie almost never called her at work.

"I just quit my job," Carrie said.

"Good for you."

Her mother's reaction surprised her. "You don't think I was being too rash?"

"I think it's long overdue. Those chauvinists are never going to give you the credit you deserve."

"You never said anything."

"It wasn't my place, but now that you've done it, I think you made the right decision."

"I think I'm going to open my own business," she said. "Try to find some clients."

"That's an excellent idea."

"It will probably take me a while to get off the ground and make any money."

"I have savings. We'll be fine."

Her mother sounded so calm and confident. She made Carrie feel that way, too. "Thanks," she said. "I just wanted to let you know. I have to go write my resignation letter now."

"Don't let them talk you out of this," Becky said. "It's really for the best."

Abernathy didn't try to talk her out of it, and Vance didn't even bother to stop by her desk to say goodbye. Carrie left her letter of resignation on Abernathy's desk, then packed her belongings in a box that had once held copy paper and left under the curious eyes of a few clerks and the receptionist. "Good luck," the receptionist, Lynn, said, and flashed a brief smile.

Carrie loaded the box into the back of her SUV, then sat in the driver's seat, shaky and a little lightheaded. She was elated and terrified, mind spinning with plans for the future. She would need to find office space, but it didn't have to be anything big or fancy. She could contact the local real estate companies and contractors, and let them know she was available to design new construction or additions. She would need to register her business, open a bank account, maybe take out an ad in the paper. She needed a business plan and a budget. Should she talk to the bank about a line of credit?

She dug a notepad from her purse and began making a list, energized by all the ideas flooding her brain. She was so lost in her plans she didn't register her ringing phone at first. The call was from emergency dispatch.

"Hello, Carrie," Rayanne's pleasant voice said. "We just received a call about a climber fallen in Horse Thief Canyon. Near Mile Marker 6, where County Road 31 parallels the gorge."

Carrie made note of the location on her pad. "Who called it in?" she asked. "What did they say?"

"They didn't leave a name and they weren't on the line long enough for our system to register the number. Either that or they were calling from a phone with blocking software or something. Sorry I don't have more for you. The sheriff's department is responding, so there should be an officer to meet you there."

"Thanks, Rayanne." Carrie ended the call and immediately started typing a text to the other volunteers. As many as were available would respond. As she entered the location information, she realized this was very close to where they had been training the day Tony was injured. A shudder went through her at the memory.

She hit Send, then turned the key in the ignition, intending to drive to search and rescue headquarters. But before she could pull away from the curb, her phone rang again, with a call from Austen.

"Hello, Carrie?" Austen sounded out of breath. "I need your help."

The real fear in his voice startled her. "Austen, what's wrong?"

"I got the text about the fallen climber and I realized I was right here," he said. "I mean, I was less than a mile away. Now I'm here at the location and I don't know what to do. I can hear someone down there. Someone screaming." His voice broke. "I think they're really hurt. I don't know what to do."

"It's okay," she said. "Just…calm down. Wait for the rest of the crew to arrive. Remember, we're a team. Wait for the team. We'll be there soon."

"Can you come right now?" he asked. "I don't have enough experience to handle this. It's freaking me out."

"I'm on my way to SAR headquarters now." She shifted into gear and checked her mirrors before pulling out into the empty street.

"Please, could you come now? The rest of the team will get the supplies we need. I'm sorry to be so much trouble, but I'd really appreciate it if you'd come."

He really did sound desperate. She thought back to her own early days with SAR. Being alone at the scene with a hurting person would have shaken her up, too. "All right," she said. "I have to change clothes, then I'll be right there."

DANNY WAS THREE hours into his shift when he got the text about the fallen climber. Helene saw him checking his phone. "Is it a search and rescue call?" she asked.

"A climber has fallen in Horse Thief Canyon," he said.

"We're slow today," Helene said. "You should go."

It was true they didn't have a full schedule today,

and he had an informal agreement that allowed him to respond to SAR calls if there was enough staff to cover for him. "Thanks," he said, and headed for his car. He hit his emergency flashers and set out. He would need to stop by SAR headquarters for his full medical pack, which would eat up more time, but he would still arrive in time to back up Hannah for any needed medical care.

The drive from Delta took twenty-five minutes. He was surprised to find the parking lot at SAR headquarters full of vehicles when he arrived. He recognized Hannah's Toyota and Sheri's Subaru, along with several other volunteers' cars. Most of them should have left for the accident scene by now. He hurried to the side door and tried to open it, but it refused to budge.

He pounded on the door. "Hey! Somebody let me in."

Moments later, he heard footsteps approaching. Sheri's face appeared in the small window at the top of the door. "The door is jammed," she said. "Or there's something wrong with the lock. Can you open it from the outside?"

He tried again. "No. What's going on? Why is everyone still here?"

"There's something wrong with the doors," Sheri said. "We got in okay, but now we can't get out."

Was this the work of the person who had been targeting them? "Did you call for help?" he asked. Did they need a locksmith? Or the sheriff?

"Our phones aren't working, either," Sheri said.

Danny pulled his phone from his pocket. The screen showed No Signal, which didn't make any sense. Was a transmitter down somewhere?

Ryan took Sheri's place at the door. "We think something is jamming the phone signal," he said.

This was sounding more sinister by the second. "Where's Carrie?" Danny asked.

"She went straight to the scene." Sheri again. "She said she was meeting Austen there."

"Why didn't Austen come here first?" Danny asked. As a trainee, he wasn't going to be able to do much at the scene by himself.

"I don't know," Sheri said. "Carrie just texted that she was meeting him there."

"So Carrie is alone at the scene with Austen?" Fear was quickly overtaking confusion.

"The sheriff's department was sending a deputy," Sheri said. "I'm so glad you showed up. You're going to have to go for help."

"I'll call someone," he said, and turned away. But he'd do it while headed for Horse Thief Canyon. He had a bad feeling about this.

Chapter Sixteen

The flashing lights of a sheriff's department cruiser marked the location of the accident on County Road 31. Carrie slowed and parked behind Austen's truck in the pullout a short distance from the cruiser. She had stopped at her house long enough to change into technical pants, boots, and a fleece top. Austen was dressed much the same as he trotted toward her down the roadside. "Thanks for coming," he said. "The poor guy is still carrying on down there. I'm really worried about him."

He took her arm and tugged her toward a wider pullout, beyond the cruiser, where she could see ropes beside an anchor, and other climbing gear. "Some of this is my stuff, but most of it was already here when I arrived," Austen explained. "I guess it belongs to the guy who fell."

She looked around them. "Where's the deputy?"

"He walked up the road a ways to try to get a better phone signal." Austen pointed down into the canyon. "I can't see the guy who fell, but from the sound of him, I think he's just below us."

Just then, a scream of agony sent every hair standing up on the back of Carrie's neck. "Has he been doing that since you got here?" she asked.

"Yeah. It's just terrible. I tried shouting down that help was on its way, but I don't know if he can hear me."

"Was he climbing by himself?" She studied the ropes. There were two sets arranged twenty feet apart, but Austen had said one of them belonged to him.

"I don't know," Austen said. "There was only one set of gear when I got here, but maybe whoever he was with panicked and left. Maybe that's who called in the accident."

"You would think he would stay with his friend," she said.

"I guess everyone reacts differently in a crises," Austen said.

The man down in the canyon screamed again, the sound echoing off the rock walls. Carrie cringed. She told herself it was a good sign that he still had the strength to cry out that way, but he must be terribly injured to be in so much pain. "One of us should go down there and see if there's something we can do to make him more comfortable until the others get here," Austen said.

"We don't have any medical supplies," she said. "Hannah or Danny should be here soon." She looked down the road, hoping to spot someone approaching. But the pavement was empty, the only movement the flashing lights of the cruiser. "Who was the deputy who responded?" she asked. If it was Jake, he was one more trained person she could count on.

"A reserve officer, I think," Austen said. "Nobody I know."

Carrie pulled out her phone as the man in the canyon let out another strangled cry. "Help! Won't somebody help?"

She checked the time—11:30 a.m. Half an hour since she had texted the call to SAR volunteers. Headquarters was only about fifteen minutes away. Say, five or ten minutes there to assemble their gear. Ten or fifteen minutes before that for people to start arriving at headquarters. "The first volunteers should be here any second now," she said.

"If you go on down to the injured man, I can watch from up here," Austen said. "The deputy should be back soon, too, and he can help."

"I'm not going to be able to do anything when I get down there," Carrie protested. "And one of our more experienced climbers, like Sheri or Ryan, will be able to get down there much faster."

Another wail, primal in its terror, cut off her words. "We can't just let him suffer," Austen said. He picked up the pack next to the coils of climbing rope. "I have some medical stuff in here—bandages and splints and a neck brace. Warming packs and stuff like that. He's probably going into shock. At least you could get him warm and stabilized." He slipped on the pack. "If you're too scared to go down there, I'll do it."

"I'm not scared. It's just not proper procedure."

"I think alleviating someone's pain—and possibly saving their life—comes ahead of any procedure,"

Austen said. "Especially when the others will be here any minute."

She turned away from him, toward the sound of an approaching car, spirits lifting. The gray SUV slowed for the curve, then sped up, past the sheriff's cruiser, on down the road. Not one of the SAR volunteers. Carrie's stomach twisted as the man below began sobbing and pleading with them again. "All right, I'll go down." Anything to stop that poor man's crying. And Austen was right. Shock was a real danger with injuries like these. Getting him warm now might make the difference between him living and dying.

"Use my gear." Austen handed her a harness and climbing helmet.

Carrie stepped into the harness, then put on the gear. She fastened her personal anchor system to the anchors drilled into the rock, double-checking that it was secure. Austen handed her the climbing rope and she tied an overhand knot in one end and clipped this to her harness with a carabiner. Then she threaded the other end of the rope through the rappel rings on the anchors and pulled until the center of the line was in the rings. She gathered the ends of the rope together and tied a stopper knot, pulling hard to make sure it was secure. She clipped her belay device to the rope and to her harness, then unclipped and untied the overhand knot she had made earlier.

"That all looks good," Austen said. "You're ready to go."

She glanced toward the road once more. "I don't understand why no one else is here yet."

"I'm sure they'll be here soon," Austen said, his last words almost drowned out as the man below screamed again. "You'd better get going."

She nodded, then took a deep breath and tossed the rope into the canyon. It uncoiled gracefully, falling free of obstacles. She leaned back to make sure her harness and anchors were secure, checked that the rope below her was even, with stopper knots in both ends. So much of climbing safety was about double-checking and triple checking. When she was satisfied everything was as secure as she could make it, she unclipped her personal anchoring system from the fixed anchors and took her first step backward into the canyon. She kept firm hold on the prussic loop, using it to provide friction to slowly lower herself down. At the same time, she was listening for the arrival of anyone overhead.

"You're doing great," Austen called when she was about ten feet down. "But hurry. Our climber has gotten awfully quiet down there."

It was true there was no longer any noise from the canyon below. Had he lost consciousness, or worse, was he dead? She pushed the thought away and focused on descending into the canyon. For her, that was the only way to get through this task. She needed to concentrate on doing everything exactly as she had been taught. She had to keep herself safe in order to reach the bottom safely, where she could help the person who needed her.

She lowered another ten feet, then some noise at the canyon rim, or maybe some movement of the rope, made her look up. She couldn't see Austen anymore. Had he moved away, or was he simply out of sight because of the angle of her body now? "Austen?" she called.

No answer. A chill went through her. She told herself she was being foolish. Maybe the others had arrived and he had gone to greet them. She couldn't hear anything, but all this rock around her was probably blocking noise.

She continued her slow descent. She wanted to look down and see if she could spot the injured man, but she knew from experience that looking down was a bad idea. She had never been the first to rappel into a canyon before. Every other time she had done this, someone had been waiting at the bottom to steady her as she arrived and help her unclip. She looked to her left, to gauge how much farther she had to go, and was dismayed to see that she was only about halfway through her descent. She had always envied other climbers, like Tony and Sheri, who seemed to float down, descending rapidly and easily. For her, every rappel was an exercise of physical and mental will.

"How are you doing?"

She looked up and was relieved to see Austen, leaning over to look down at her. "I'm good," she called up. "Halfway there."

"It's a long way to fall," he said.

Was that his idea of a joke? "I'm not going to fall!" she shouted up at him. "Is anyone else there yet?"

"They won't be coming," he said. "It's just you and me."

"Of course they're coming!" she said. Why was he behaving so oddly? "Quit making stupid jokes."

"It's not a joke. Not a joke at all." He held something out in his hand. "I'll say goodbye now, Carrie. I have to leave soon."

"What are you talking about? Austen, stop it!" He was frightening her now.

"This is a bottle of acid," he said. "I'm going to pour it on the ropes. The whole thing, not just a little, like I did with Tony. You might be able to climb a little farther down before the ropes give way, but I doubt it."

His words had the effect of drenching, icy water. She couldn't breathe, and she couldn't move. *He* was the one who had tried to kill Tony? The one who had destroyed the Beast and hidden the Jaws and everything else that had plagued them. "I thought you loved search and rescue!" she shouted. "Why would you do this?"

"I loved Julie," he said. "Search and rescue was supposed to save her, but you didn't. I can't bring Julie back, but I can make you pay for her death."

She wanted to argue that they had done everything in their power to save his fiancée. She had simply been too badly injured to recover. And they had worked to save Austen's own life. But she knew there was no sense trying to reason with a man who would pour acid on a climber's ropes. "Austen, don't do this!" she said instead.

"Goodbye, Carrie," he said, and moved the container of acid closer to the ropes.

Danny scrolled through the directory on his phone until he found Jake's direct number, then hit the call button as he started the engine in his car. The call didn't go through on his first attempt, but as he sped back toward town, his cell signal returned and the phone began to ring. "Hello?" Jake answered.

"Jake, it's Danny. Someone rigged all the doors at search and rescue headquarters, and the other volunteers are trapped inside. Their phones won't work, either."

"Where are you now?" Jake asked.

"I'm on my way to Horse Thief Canyon."

"I got the text about a climbing accident there," Jake said.

"Right," Danny said. "The others had reported to headquarters to get their gear to respond to that call when they ended up trapped inside. I was coming from Delta, so I arrived after everyone else. But Carrie got a call from Austen asking her to meet him at the scene, so she bypassed headquarters and drove straight there. She's alone at the scene with Austen and that has me worried."

"Because you think Austen might be the person behind the previous attacks on SAR?" Jake asked.

"I don't know," Danny said. "But the whole situation is wrong—the other volunteers being trapped at headquarters and Carrie and Austen alone at the scene of an accident. Maybe both of them are in danger."

"I'm patrolling in the southern part of the county," Jake said. About as far from Horse Thief Canyon as he could get, Danny thought. "Hang on a minute," Jake said. "I'm going to contact the deputy we sent to the accident site."

Danny focused on driving, one hand clutching the steering wheel, the other his phone as he waited, trying not to think of all the things that could be happening with Carrie and Austen. Was Austen the person behind all the attacks on SAR? He and Carrie had both thought he was too dedicated, and too new to the group to have developed any grievances. "Danny?" Jake asked.

"I'm here."

"I can't raise the deputy. He's not responding to the radio. I'm going to head over there, but it's going to take me at least twenty minutes to get there."

"Could you send someone to get the other volunteers out of search and rescue headquarters?" Danny asked. "I should be at Horse Thief in a few minutes."

"Wait for law enforcement," Jake said. "If Austen or someone else on the scene is behind all of this, you shouldn't confront them."

Danny nodded. What Jake said made perfect sense. Except that Carrie was in danger. He wasn't going to sit on his hands and do nothing if that was the case. "I'll be careful," he said. "But I'm not going to let anyone hurt Carrie." He ended the call and tossed the phone into the passenger seat. It rang again almost immediately, but he ignored it.

He thought back over the events of the past month. Austen had been one of the people helping with the climbing gear the day Tony was injured. Could he have poured acid on the ropes without anyone noticing? He could have come back to headquarters that night and burned the Beast. They had dismissed him as a suspect because he had been attacked himself the next day. But what if he had faked that accident to deflect suspicion? His injury wasn't that bad, and it would have been easy enough to let his truck slide into the ditch and bang his head against the door frame. Austen could have hidden the Jaws in the boiler room. He could have even slashed Carrie's tires.

Danny slapped his hand on the steering wheel as yet another realization hit him. Austen had been working the booth at the fair when the contributions went missing. All he had to do was wait until Sheri was busy talking with someone and he could have taken the money.

They had been so fixated on Ted as the most likely culprit he hadn't considered the rookie. Ted was angry and didn't hide his feelings. What if Austen had come into the group with a grudge and bided his time until he could get his revenge? Maybe his dedication was only an act.

What was the best way to approach this? If he roared up in his car, he might startle Austen—or someone else, if Austen was innocent—into doing something stupid, something that would hurt Carrie. What had happened to the deputy? Was Austen planning another prank, like hiding the Jaws and slashing Carrie's tires, or did he have something more dangerous in mind? The man was clearly unpredictable. Danny would have to be smart, and careful.

He spotted the emergency lights of a sheriff's department cruiser ahead and slowed, then pulled to the side of the road, several hundred yards from the cruiser. He pocketed his phone, then searched for some kind of weapon. Nothing. The first aid kit probably had scissors, but he didn't plan to get close enough to Austen for them to be effective. The only thing in his favor was that he was a lot taller and maybe stronger than the other man. And he wasn't unhinged by whatever motive had led Austen to want to hurt the organization that had first saved his life, then welcomed him as one of their own.

Maybe he was wrong. Maybe Austen was innocent and there was nothing going on here but two search and rescue volunteers trying to save an injured climber. If that was the case, Danny wouldn't need to do anything but pitch in and help. But being cautious wouldn't hurt anything.

He crossed the road and moved into the cover of trees, trying to assess the situation. The sheriff's cruiser sat empty, the red-and-blue lights silently flashing. He couldn't see anyone inside or near the vehicle. Just past it, Carrie's SUV sat behind Austen's truck in a pullout. And past that, there was Austen. He crouched on the ground next to the rim of the canyon. What was he doing down there?

Heart in his throat, Danny watched from behind a scrubby piñon. Where was Carrie? His gaze fixed on the lines coiled next to Austen, and anchors sticking up from the rock, and with a sickening plummet of his stomach, he realized Carrie must be on the end of the rope. Austen was doing something to them. Was he going to cut through them? No, that wasn't a knife in his hand. It looked like a bottle.

"No!" The word tore from Danny's throat, and he hurtled from the trees and crossed the road at a run.

Austen looked up, then half rose. "Stop right there!" he shouted. "Stop now, or I'll dump all this acid right on top of her."

Danny skidded to a halt, sending a shower of gravel into the canyon below. "Get away from her!" he shouted.

Austen shook his head. "It's too late for that. And don't think you can stop me. If you try to tackle me now, you'll send us both into the canyon. I don't think you want that."

"Danny, no!" He recognized Carrie's voice, from deep in the canyon.

"Are you all right?" Danny called, then decided this was a stupid question. How "all right" could she be with Austen threatening her?

"You need to leave," Austen said.

Danny glared at him. "You poured that acid on Tony's climbing ropes," he said.

"I didn't use enough," Austen said. "I won't make that mistake this time." He tilted the bottle over Carrie's ropes.

"No!" But it was too late. The acid cascaded over the twined fiber, sending up an acrid stench. Danny knotted his fists, shaking with rage and the frustration of not being able to do anything to help.

The sound of a car door slamming echoed around

them like a gunshot. Austen's head jerked in the direction of the sound and he swore.

Danny took advantage of that brief distraction to act. He rushed forward, but instead of pushing Austen, he grabbed him and dragged him away from the canyon rim. Austen fought like a wildcat. He had dropped the acid bottle, but he scratched at Danny's face, kicked him and tried to gouge his eyes. Danny dodged the blows and succeeded in punching the shorter man in the stomach, hard, knocking the wind out of him. Then he forced him to the ground and began pummeling him, determined to beat him into submission.

Strong arms pulled Danny off the now-subdued Austen. "It's okay." Jake patted Danny's back. "Calm down."

Danny nodded and drew in a shaky breath. Austen lay on his stomach on the ground, Deputy Dwight Prentice fastening his hands with flex-cuffs.

"You okay now?" Jake asked.

"Yes."

Jake released him, and Danny immediately turned toward the canyon. "Carrie!" he shouted, and ran to kneel beside the ropes. "Austen poured acid on her climbing ropes." He stared at the spot where he could see the acid had eaten into the rope, weakening the fibers.

"What's going on up there?" Carrie called up, her voice taut with fear.

Danny lay on his stomach and extended head and shoulders over the edge until he could see Carrie.

She stared up at him, white-faced beneath an orange climbing helmet. "Is there a ledge, or any kind of hand- and foothold?" he called. "Anywhere you can take some weight off the rope?"

She looked around. "There's a little tree growing out of the rock."

"Do you think it will hold your weight?" Danny asked.

"Maybe."

"Get over to it and tie off on it," Danny said. "I'm going to come down and get you."

A second set of ropes was tied into a pair of anchors twenty yards to the left. He pulled at the rope and it came up easily. Jake moved to help him, and together they brought up the rope. "Is there an injured climber down there?" Jake asked.

"I don't know," Danny said. "But we've got to get to Carrie."

"You don't have any climbing gear," Jake said.

Danny looked down into the canyon. Someone like Ryan or Tony might have been able to free climb down, but he didn't have that kind of experience. "How are you doing, Carrie?" he called.

"I'm tied off on the tree," she said. Was it his imagination or did she sound calmer? "I think it's going to hold."

"We're going to get to you as soon as we can."

A horn honked and he whipped around to see Sheri's Jeep pulling in behind Carrie's SUV. Sheri, Eldon, Hannah and Ryan spilled out of the vehicle.

Danny stood. "Did you bring climbing gear?" he called.

"Of course," Ryan said, and turned to pull ropes and harnesses from the vehicle.

"What's the situation?" Sheri jogged up to join them. She stared at Austen, still prone on the ground, a grim-faced Dwight standing over him.

"Austen poured acid on Carrie's climbing ropes," Danny said. "She's tied off on a tree about halfway down the canyon, but we've got to get to her."

Sheri nodded, then turned to Ryan, who had approached, coils of rope over his shoulder. While the two of them conferred, Danny turned to Eldon. "How did the rest of you get out?"

"Gage Walker showed up and busted in the door." Eldon grinned. "It was like something out of a movie."

A movie Danny wouldn't have wanted to see. Eldon nodded to Austen. "What's with him?"

"He's the one who tried to hurt Tony and burned the Beast and everything else," Danny said. "He tried to kill Carrie."

Eldon's eyes widened. "Why did he do that?"

"I don't know." Danny closed his eyes. He didn't even care why Austen had acted the way he had. All he wanted was for Carrie to be safe.

But for the next half hour, all he could do was wait while Sheri, Ryan and Eldon worked to descend into the canyon to where Carrie waited. Long minutes later, she emerged on top once more. "I'm okay," she said as the others swarmed around her. "It was terrifying, but I'm okay." She smiled at Danny and his knees felt weak. He held out his arms and she came to him and he pulled her close, not even caring that the others were watching.

But their moment of closeness lasted only a few seconds. She pulled away and resumed the role of captain. “Someone needs to get down into the canyon and see about the injured climber,” she said.

“Sheri is headed down,” Ryan said.

“Are you sure someone is down there?” Danny asked.

“Someone was down there, screaming in agony.” Carrie bit her lower lip. “They haven’t said anything in a long time. We may be too late.”

More cops arrived, along with an ambulance and a newspaper reporter. Austen was put into Dwight’s cruiser and driven away. “He blamed us for his fiancée’s death,” Carrie said. “He wanted revenge on all of us for her dying. Joining SAR was just a way to get back at the team.”

“That doesn’t even make sense,” Eldon said.

“These kind of things usually don’t.” Jake said.

Sheri radioed from the bottom of the canyon. “There’s no one down here,” she said. “But there is a big tape recorder with speakers.”

“I guess that’s what I heard,” Carrie said. “A recording of an injured person.”

“Austen must have been the anonymous caller who reported the fallen climber,” Jake said. He gestured to the ropes in the anchors. “He set up all this with the recorder in the canyon to fool you.”

“The pleas for help on the recording were so

awful," Carrie said. "Anyone would have wanted to help a person who was suffering that much."

"That's what he was counting on." Danny put his arm around her again and she leaned against him.

"The locks on all the doors at search and rescue headquarters had been tampered with," Gage said. "And he probably planted some kind of cell phone signal blocker in the building. You can buy them off the internet."

"He sure went to a lot of trouble," Ryan said. "It's like something out of a spy thriller—jammed door locks and cell phone signal blockers. And he had to climb down into the canyon to set up that recorder, then climb back up on his own."

"I think he had been planning all of this a long time," Jake said.

"What happened to the deputy?" Carrie asked. "The one who first responded to the call?"

"Austen hit him on the head, probably with a rock, and probably when his back was turned," Gage said. "Then he tied him up, gagged him and locked him in the trunk of the cruiser. He's on his way to the hospital to be checked out, but he should be okay." He put a hand on Carrie's shoulder. "What about you? Do you need to be examined?"

"I'm fine. Just…a little shaken up."

"You should go home," Ryan said. "The rest of us can finish up here."

She straightened her shoulders. "I'm still captain. I'm not going to leave the rest of the team behind."

"You should let them mop up here," Gage said. "We need you and Danny to come to the sheriff's department and give a statement." His eyes met Danny's over Carrie's head. "The sooner, the better."

Carrie insisted on driving herself to the Rayford County sheriff's office. Danny followed, his gaze continually returning to the back of her head, his mind bouncing between relief that she was all right, and the terrible image of what might have happened.

CARRIE GOT THROUGH the next hour on automatic pilot. She had no memory of the drive to the sheriff's department, and couldn't have told anyone later what she said in the interview with Deputy Dwight Prentice. She told him everything that had happened from the moment she received the call from the emergency dispatcher until she arrived safely at the top of the canyon, the events playing out in her mind like a movie trailer—the way Austen looked so normal as he encouraged her to help the man in pain at the bottom of the canyon, and the wild edge to his voice as he talked about pouring acid on the climbing ropes and sending her plummeting to her death. "He always seemed so ordinary," she said. "He wasn't angry or resentful or anything like that. I trusted him."

"There was no reason you shouldn't have," Dwight said. "For what it's worth, none of us suspected him, either. He did a good job of not leaving evidence behind."

Finally, they released her and she found Danny

waiting for her in the little lobby of the sheriff's department. He pulled her close and she rested her head against his shoulder and closed her eyes. She could have stayed there all afternoon, but after a few minutes, she began to feel awkward. She looked up at him. "Want to hear something funny?" she asked.

"What's that?"

"I quit my job this morning. I thought that would be the thing I remembered most about this day."

"Let's get a cup of coffee," he said.

She followed him to his car and she thought he would drive to a coffee shop. Instead, he drove to his apartment. They climbed the stairs to the four rooms over a T-shirt shop and he fed coffee pods into a machine and poured two cups. Then he sat at his small kitchen table across from her. "How are you doing?" he asked.

"I'm okay." She took a sip of coffee and felt its warmth spread through her. "Getting better every minute."

"Yeah." He stared at the tabletop, both hands wrapped around his mug, but made no move to drink. "I'm still shaking inside," he said. "I've never been so terrified in my life."

"Oh, Danny." She leaned over and put a hand on his. "It's okay."

He squeezed his eyes shut and nodded. Alarmed, she thought she saw tears. She wanted to reassure him again, but she couldn't find her voice, so moved by the depth of his emotion.

He drew in a deep breath, then finally took a sip of coffee. When he set the cup down again, he looked calmer. Able to look her in the eye. "I don't do commitment," he said. "I can't. I always end up holding back, and hurting people I don't want to hurt."

Was he telling her this as a prelude to breaking up with her? She didn't read it that way. "Is that because of your parents?" she asked. A mother who was mentally ill probably hadn't been able to be there for her children. And it sounded like he spent a lot of time taking care of her now.

"It doesn't take a genius to figure that out," he said. "I guess if you find out at an early age you can't count on the people who are supposed to look after you, it warps you somehow."

"I don't think you're warped," she said. "You spend your life looking after other people. You risk your life to take care of people you don't even know as part of search and rescue." And he dropped everything to take care of the mother who had never really taken care of him.

"Yeah, well, I guess we all try to fill in the gaps in our lives."

Was rescue work her way of filling the gaps—of trying to redeem her failed marriage and her stifled career? "Why are you telling me this?" she asked. It was the kind of intimate confession she wasn't sure she would have had the courage to share.

He took another deep breath, and let it out slowly, like a weightlifter preparing to hoist a heavy burden.

"I'm telling you because you make me think about the long-term—sticking with you. That maybe this time I could do it." His eyes met hers. "I'm warning you, I guess. It feels like a big risk."

Her heart pounded, a dull ache in her chest. She rubbed at the spot, trying to massage away the sensation. To push down the mix of fear and elation. "You know how much I don't like climbing," she said. After today, it certainly wouldn't be any easier.

He nodded, eyes questioning.

"But I do it anyway," she said. "Because I know it's important. And I believe it will make a difference." She wrapped both her hands over his. "Some risks are worth taking, no matter how scary they are." She leaned closer. "I think we're worth the risk, don't you?"

His lips met hers in a crushing kiss, equal parts desperation and passion. She stood up and wrapped her arms around him and tasted salt, and didn't know if the tears were hers or his. She was alive. She was with the man she loved, who loved her in return. Everything else seemed minor compared to that reality.

He broke the kiss and stared into her eyes. "Do you really think we can do this?"

"Yes," she whispered, then more firmly. "Yes."

He kissed her again. Somewhere a phone rang. His? Hers? "Do you need to answer that?" he asked, his lips still pressed to hers.

"In a minute," she said. She was going to enjoy this a little bit longer. Right now she was exactly where she needed to be. Where she wanted to be, maybe even for the rest of her life. The thought wasn't as scary as she expected. Maybe finding the right person was like that—like a secure anchor you could count on to never let you down.

Epilogue

"It's time, everyone!" Sheri stepped forward and raised a beribboned champagne bottle. Smiling for the cameras, she brought the bottle to rest against the hood of the bright yellow rescue vehicle parked in front of the search and rescue headquarters. "I hereby christen you Beast Two!"

Carrie joined the crowd in cheering. Two months had passed since the terrible day in the canyon, and search and rescue had rebounded from that near tragedy. In addition to a new Beast, they had three new trainees. Tony was back on limited duty, and even Ted had moved into the new role of historian. He was working on his book, combing through the archives and interviewing past and present volunteers for stories of rescues.

Sheri had been elected the new SAR captain after Carrie had declined to continue in the role. She had a new business to get off the ground, and a new relationship to tend to. She looked across at Danny, who was opening bottles of champagne to distribute among the attendees. Things were going so well with the two of them. She had thought it would be difficult to adjust to having someone in her life constantly, but Danny and she had meshed so easily. The two of them were looking for a house together, while Becky planned to get her own place nearby. His new supervisory position at the surgical center had given him a new enthusiasm for his work as well as an increase in pay that would help them afford a mortgage. Dylan and Amber were excited, too, about the new house, and about Danny being a part of their lives.

"You look happy." Danny joined her, and handed her a glass of champagne.

"I am happy." Happier than she could remember being.

"I talked to Jake just now," he said. "He says the judge has finally set a trial date for Austen."

"That's good." She sipped the champagne. Austen had been charged with two counts of attempted murder and one of arson as well as theft of funds from a nonprofit. He had relocated to Denver while he awaited trial, but the sheriff's office seemed to think they had a solid case against him. Files on his computer showed he had been planning the crimes for months.

"We'll probably both have to testify," Danny said. "Are you okay with that?"

"A little nervous, but it's nothing I can't handle." That was her approach to life these days. Instead of avoiding things that felt scary or uncomfortable, she was forging ahead. She had been climbing three times since the accident, each a little less nerve-wracking than the time before. And she had worked up the nerve to approach contractors and real estate agents, resulting in almost more business than she could handle. She had been able to hire an administrative assistant and was thinking of taking on an intern.

Danny put his arm around her shoulders. “You inspire me,” he said.

This wasn’t the first time he had said this, and as compliments went, she thought it was her favorite. She had come a long way from the woman whose voice shook the first time she had to address a search and rescue meeting. With Danny by her side, they would both go a lot further.

* * * * *

COMING NEXT MONTH FROM

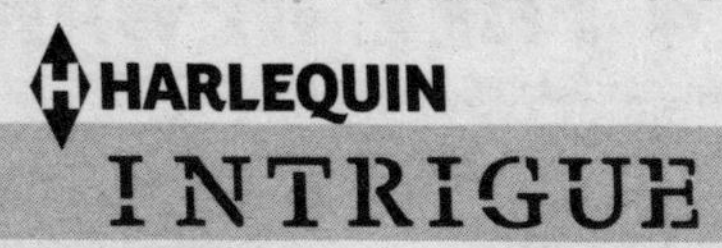

#2127 CONARD COUNTY: K-9 DETECTIVES
Conard County: The Next Generation • by Rachel Lee
Veterans Jenna Blair and Kell McLaren have little in common. But when they join forces to solve a local murder with the help of Kell's K-9 companion, they uncover a web of danger that requires them to reevaluate their partnership...and their growing feelings for one another.

#2128 ONE NIGHT STANDOFF
Covert Cowboy Soldiers • by Nicole Helm
When Hazeleigh Hart finds her boss's murdered body, she runs...directly into rancher Landon Thompson. He vows to help clear her name—he knows she's no murderess. But will their hideout be discovered by the killer before Hazeleigh is exonerated?

#2129 TEXAS BODYGUARD: LUKE
San Antonio Security • by Janie Crouch
Claire Wallace has stumbled upon corporate espionage—and murder. Now the software engineer is being framed for both crimes. Security expert Luke Patterson protected her in the past and he'll risk it all to do it again. But is the real culprit already one step ahead of them?

#2130 DANGER ON MAUI
Hawaii CI • by R. Barri Flowers
Murders, stalkers and serial killers! It's all fair game in the world of true crime writer Daphne Dockery. But when life imitates art, she'll need Hawaiian homicide detective Kenneth Kealoha to protect her from becoming the next victim in her repertoire.

#2131 FRENCH QUARTER FATALE
by Joanna Wayne
FBI terrorist special agent Keenan Carter knows nothing about being a famous actress's daughter. That doesn't diminish his attraction to Josette Guillory...or his determination to protect her from the assassin targeting her for her inheritance. If only they could locate her missing mother to get to the truth...

#2132 GOING ROGUE IN RED RYE COUNTY
Secure One • by Katie Mettner
Dirty cops sabotaged FBI Agent Mini August's latest operation and left her on the run for her life. But when Special Agent Roman Jacobs finds his injured, compromised ex-partner in a North Dakota forest, will he risk his badge to help her...or finish the job her target started?

YOU CAN FIND MORE INFORMATION ON UPCOMING HARLEQUIN TITLES, FREE EXCERPTS AND MORE AT HARLEQUIN.COM.

HICNM0123